Murder Mistress

Robert Colby

PROLOGUE BOOKS

F + W Media, Inc.

Published in electronic format by
PROLOGUE BOOKS
an imprint of F+W Media, Inc.
10151 Carver Road
Blue Ash, Ohio 45242
www.prologuebooks.com

eISBN 10: 1-4405-3714-3
eISBN 13: 978-1-4405-3714-1
POD ISBN 10: 1-4405-5518-4
POD ISBN 13: 978-1-4405-55518-3

This is a work of fiction. Names, characters, corporations, institutions,
organizations, events, or locales in this novel are either the product of the author's
imagination or, if real, used fictitiously. The resemblance of any character to actual
persons (living or dead) is entirely coincidental.

This work has been previously published in print format by:
Ace Books, Inc.

COME AND SLAY WITH ME

Driving to Miami, Scott Daniels paused to rescue a lady in distress. She was in a road house, abandoned by her date, and so Scott offered Valerie a lift. No sooner had they started off, then they spotted the boy friend's car smashed in an accident.

Valerie begged Scott to save her good name by salvaging her suitcase from the wreck before the cops could find it. But no sooner had he done so, then he learned that instead of being filled with pink unmentionables, it was loaded with green negotiables—hundreds of thousands of them!

Curiosity being stronger than caution, Scott kept his eye on Valerie after dropping her off in Miami. And thus found himself the only element remaining between a gang of ruthless criminals and the perfect crime.

Turn this book over for second complete novel

CAST OF CHARACTERS

Scott Daniels

Success had not passed him by, it had run him down.

Valerie McLean

Her one weakness was money. She always paid inflationary prices for it!

Myra Daniels

Myra cared about what Scott was, not how much he made.

Roy Whalen

Securing his own pleasure cashed him in.

Clay Schofield

Being a banker, he knew all about high finance and fancy bookwork.

Marty Bates

Marty was dead, which was why he offered so much self-convicting evidence.

ONE

At ten o'clock that night, Scott Daniels estimated that he was about two hours out of Miami. He had been driving south since dawn with only the dashboard radio for company. In the afternoon, the heat of a merciless July hot spell had begun to wear him down so that the landscape fused and shimmered and the hours of road-jog made him feel strangely unbalanced and light-headed.

He had spun across the middle of the state over Route 27 because the towns were fewer and smaller and he could make better time. Also, there were long stretches of open road such as the one he was traveling now—nothing for endless miles but the flat tangle of the Everglades. He had stopped only once to eat—grabbing a quick sandwich while the car was being gassed and checked.

His haste was not of necessity. He had another six days of vacation and tomorrow would be just a span of idleness with depressing reflections over his failure in New York. But Myra waited in the stuffy little westside apartment. And while Myra waited he wasn't going to spend another night on the road. Because as his whole bright and hectic success had come tumbling down in a fraction of the time it took to build it, Myra had stood on the sidelines with a certain sadness in her smile but without the least accusation in her eyes. And above all in the world that was left to him, he loved Myra most. So that the urgency which pushed him forward into the night against hunger, against bone weariness, was self-induced.

A half hour earlier the heat had reached a seemingly inevitable climax in one of those massive, broken-dam thundershowers for which Florida is famous. The rain had come smashing out of the sky as though driven by a minor

5

hurricane, visibility had been not much better than a car length ahead, the road was practically awash and Daniels had lost the better part of twenty minutes before abruptly, it ended. Now the highway glistened under the long cone of his headlights, the air which rushed past his window was only slightly cooler and there was a soggy smell and feel to it. Yet, in one sense, Daniels was revived and eager—it was a mere spurt to Miami.

He hadn't seen a half dozen cars in the last forty minutes, not a single habitation. A lone gas station had been closed. But just ahead there was an intersection where he knew the highway picked up a branch that curved left towards the east coast. He released the accelerator even as he saw the lights of a combined gas station and cafe. It was a long and shoddy woodframe building. White and faded-blue neon alternated, weakly blinking . . . *EATS*. . . . *GAS*. . . . *EATS*. . . . *GAS*. . . .

He needed gas. And also food. The place stood squarely to the right of the intersection and had the quality of a bleak outpost in the night. There were two pumps which sat center of an unpaved island. He wheeled his '56 Ford into position beside them and waited. When no one came he didn't blow his horn but cut the motor and lights, took the keys and went inside.

There was a rectangle of dusky room lighted by a trio of low-watt naked bulbs, suspended from ceiling cords. To one side was a scattering of scarred tables and chairs, while opposite these was a bar over which, tacked to a wall, was a hand-painted sign—*BEER AND WINE*. Next to a door which apparently led to a kitchen was a square serving window. The one touch of color in the room was an immense red-trimmed jukebox. The place had a musty wood smell, seasoned with motor oil.

A paunchy man in a stained white shirt, sleeves rolled above his biceps, leaned heavily upon the bar. He peered myopically at a crumpled newspaper as he rolled a toothpick from side to side in his mouth. If he heard Daniels, he didn't look up at his entrance.

The only other occupant of the room was an unusually attractive girl somewhere in her mid-twenties. She had dark hair which fell softly to a point just above her shoulders. Her delicately molded features were made up with that mixture of accent and restraint which come only with a natural instinct for artful grooming.

Even sitting at the bar, her long legs and the slender sweep of her waist spoke of tallness. Her white skirt seemed immaculate. She wore a pale green blouse. It was plain, short-sleeved, open at the throat and had the look of expensive silk. Strapped over her shoulder was a handsomely tooled alligator bag. Though her attire was casual, the total effect of her made her surroundings seem the more shabby.

As Daniels entered, she was already turned to face him, easing off the stool and peering at him intently, expectantly. He paused in the doorway, a little caught by the unexpected sight of such beauty apparently intent upon his arrival. Now she came towards him a step. But then as he moved and fell under the light, something went out of her face and she turned away immediately, remounting the stool and giving her undivided attention to the coffee in her cup.

The paunchy man looked up at last and said, "Something for you, mister?"

"Gas," said Daniels. "If that's in your department."

"What's that?"

"I said, fill 'er up. With regular."

"Yeah, sure thing," said the man, folding the paper and shoving it aside. "You want regular, don't ya?"

"What have you got to eat?" said Daniels, sighing and approaching the bar.

"Kitchen's closed."

Daniels frowned. "That's bad news," he said. He studied the man. "I guess it is, anyway."

"What's that?"

Daniels sat down but didn't answer.

"Got some crackers, if you're hard put. Peanut butter or cheese."

"Cheese," said Daniels. "And a beer to wash it down."

"What brand you like?"

"Just so it's cold."

The girl got off her stool and went to the open doorway, peering out. There was tension in her every movement.

"Hell of a bad rain awhile ago," said the barkeep. "God-damn skies busted wide open and fell right on top of us. You get caught in it?"

"In the middle," said Daniels absently, turning slowly to watch the girl who was still gazing out the door and pulling nervously on the strap of her bag. Nice, he thought. A sweet bundle. And right out in this wilderness—in this gas and eats joint.

There was a time, before Myra, when he would have made much of such an event. At thirty-two he was lean and darkly handsome. But two hours away, restless in the heat, Myra would be waiting. Listening for the sound of him at the door, running to comfort him, to hear him out with tender patience.

No, even if this one were willing, there was nothing in him for the old game.

The barkeep set the beer in front of him with the crackers. "Now I'll go out and gas you up," he said. "Check under the hood?"

"Just the gas," said Daniels. "And the windshield."

At the doorway the girl gave way for the man and after a final look into the darkness went to the jukebox and made much of selecting a number.

The music blared too loudly, too jarringly in the silence of the narrow room.

Still watching the machine, the girl tapped her foot. But it seemed more like a release of pressure than any real pretension of keeping time. In a minute, she came back to her stool. Tasting the cold coffee, she made a face and pushed the cup away. At that moment, she turned and their eyes met. He smiled pleasantly but without the least overtone of meaning. She smiled back, she glanced at her watch, then out the door.

It must be a guy, thought Daniels. *And I wish he'd come. I get nervous just watching her.*

The record died.

There was a rumble and the sigh of air brakes. A big trailer truck rolled to a stop on the other side of the pumps. The girl swung to the sound, startled. More on edge.than ever, she clamped teeth on lower lip and began to drum the bar surface with the pink petals of her nails. Her fingers paused, then spread out rigidly. Decision reached her face. She turned to Daniels with a set expression.

"Which way are you headed?" she said quickly.

"Miami," replied Daniels.

"On twenty-seven?"

"That's right."

"I wonder, then, if you would be willing to take me along? I seem to be stuck here." She didn't smile, offered none of the feminine charms of persuasion.

"Someone was supposed to meet you," said Daniels. "But didn't show. Is that it?"

"That's it. And, of course, I have no way to get in touch. There was a very definite arrangement and I'm worried. I must get to Miami."

"Well," said Daniels, who liked to understand the logic of a situation, "there was a storm, there are all sorts of mechanical troubles which could crop up and your friend may have been delayed. How long have you been waiting?"

She looked at her watch. "Exactly twenty-two minutes."

"Twenty-two minutes! Well, excuse me. But I really don't think you've waited long enough. People can be that late meeting you on a street corner."

She shook her head positively. "No, I'm afraid you don't understand. And I don't particularly care to explain . . . if you don't mind."

"Certainly," said Daniels. It was better not to pursue it. She seemed intelligent enough to know what she was doing. He sipped his beer.

"Can we get going?" she said. "I mean, are you ready?"

He looked at her, slightly annoyed. But he held the remark

he was about to make. There wasn't room in her face to crowd another line of disturbance. She would come apart. He gulped his beer and stood.

"I'm ready," he said. "As a matter of fact I'm in almost as much hurry as you are."

Together they went out to the car.

TWO

SHE SAT ALMOST on the edge of the seat, leaning forward slightly. Supporting herself with one hand on the dash, she peered ahead into the night.

They had gone perhaps three miles with the speedometer hovering at sixty. The highway had dried considerably and only the hiss of the tires spoke of its wetness.

"Tell me," he said. "Just as a point of curiosity, how did you arrive way out here in the first place?"

She withdrew her attention from the road with great effort and looked at him briefly. "I was brought here," she said. "By car, of course. And then the gentleman had to go alone on an errand. It wasn't supposed to take much over a minute or two. But he . . . he didn't come back."

"I see," said Daniels. "How very odd." He could understand a little better now. Though where the "gentleman" would go and on what errand in an area of the Everglades where there was nothing for miles in any direction but the gas-station-cafe, he couldn't imagine.

"I'm Scott Daniels. I never did get your name."

"Valerie," she said absently, looking straight ahead and speaking the word from the far distance of detachment.

"Valerie. . . ?" he said.

"Yes, Valerie. Just Valerie."

They lapsed into silence.

In a minute or two he became aware that he was quickly gaining on some vehicle. Far ahead he could see the red jog of a tail light. The light seemed oversized and strangely misplaced. It should be directly in line of his vision on the unbending road. But no, it appeared to wink on and off to the left. Then he picked up another blinking red eye, also to the left.

In a few seconds it was clear. They were not tail lights but signal flashers on the left side of the road. And now he could see other lights, headlights, oddly canted. It added up to an accident with police and the usual curious travelers pausing for the thrill.

He had a startling thought and looked quickly at the girl. She had seen it. She leaned forward with her face almost to the windshield. She was rigidly intent. Both hands were riveted to the dash.

"Keep calm," he said. "It could be someone else, you know. In any case, perhaps no one was hurt. You want me to stop, don't you?"

She nodded tightly without turning. "But not too close," she said in a thin, dry voice. "Please! Not too close. Stop on this side. Then you go and . . . and come back and tell me."

"Okay. Until then, just don't anticipate. It's going to be all right." But he didn't really believe it was going to be all right.

There was a side road which angled to the left. Down this road were a half dozen cars which must have pulled off the highway to avoid the narrow shoulder. And now the red flashing of patrol cars was clearly visible. And below them a small cluster of people gathered around the shadowy outlines of two automobiles which had careened off the highway into a shallow gully. The cars were separated by some twenty-five yards and one of them had keeled over.

He took the side road, parked and said, "Now—who am I looking for?"

"Never mind," she answered. "Never mind!" Her voice was on the edge of hysteria. "Just see if one of the cars is a light blue convertible with a Florida tag. It's a new Cadillac with a dark blue top. Tell me what happened to the man in it. Hurry, please. Run!"

On the highway above the wreck there were two patrol cars. An officer sat inside one of the cars and wrote something under the glow of a dome light. He paused to speak into a microphone. There was a crackling, followed by a muted reply in a heavy male voice.

Daniels looked below. A cream and red Olds sedan lay on its side like some great beast felled in a jungle. Most of the small crowd swarmed around it. A few others inspected the second car which stood upright a good seventy-five feet away. It was in shadow and the color was not distinguishable. But it appeared to be a Cadillac convertible.

Daniels stepped around to the officer's window. "Anyone hurt, officer?" he asked.

The officer gave him a hasty glance and continued writing on a sheet of paper fastened to a clipboard. "Yeah," he said. "One man hurt . . . so far."

"You don't happen to have his name there, do you?"

The officer looked up at him more carefully, then down to the sheet of paper, squinting. "Name of Martin Bates," he said. "Mean anything to ya?"

"No," said Daniels "Was he in the Olds?"

"Yup."

"Bad?"

"Don't know till we check the hospital. Ambulance took him away. Looked like he'd pull through."

"Who was in the convertible?"

"Don't know," said the officer. He pushed his cap back and sighed. "Now do me a favor and let me get this report out, will ya?"

"Sorry," said Daniels. "And thanks a lot."

He moved down into the gully and, after a brief look at the Olds, hiked over to the Cadillac. It was a late model convertible, pale blue with a dark blue top. It had Florida tags. The right front was badly mauled. Tree branches and leaves were imbedded in the broken grill. The right rear fender

was gouged, the rear bumper half torn from the body. There
was no other visible damage.

A pair of teenage boys and a young couple leaned inside
the open windows, remarking on the magnificence of the
automobile. The interior was clean and there was the smell
of new leather.

Daniels trotted up to the road and back to his car. She
was outside. Standing in the darkness.

"Tell me!" she said breathlessly. "A blue Cadillac?"

"Yes. But I don't think whoever was in it was hurt. Guy
hurt was in the Olds. You know anyone by the name of
Martin Bates?"

She let out a long breath. "No," she said. "But what about
the Cadillac?"

"The officer I talked to didn't know who was in it. No
sign of him. The other man was taken to the hospital—this
Bates."

She was silent, breathing deeply.

"I looked at the damage to the Cadillac," said Daniels.
"You don't have to worry. If your friend was hurt, it wasn't
serious. The inside is neat as a pin."

"What about the rear?" she said. "Was there any damage
to the trunk?"

"No," he said. "Why?" It seemed a curious question under
the circumstances.

"Were the keys in the switch?"

"No. I noticed they were gone."

"I have a bag in that trunk," she said. "I want that bag.
I have to get it. There are some things in it that would
identify me. I mean, I can't be associated with this man.
He's married. And there could be a scandal."

"I've got the picture," said Daniels, not terribly surprised.
"If your friend has disappeared and they tow the car in,
then. . . ."

"Exactly," she said. "So will you help me get that suitcase?"

"I don't see how," said Daniels. "I'd like to be gallant and
all that. But the trunk looked very much locked to me."

She fumbled in her purse and handed him a set of keys. He took them reluctantly.

"It's the round key," she said. "The square one is for the ignition."

"It's your car?"

"Well, no. But I used it a lot and I have my own keys."

"Great. With cops and people all over the place, I walk up and open the trunk. Don't you think someone's going to ask questions? Especially since they must be looking for this guy."

"Of course," she said, "it's possible that he took the bag with him. But just in case . . . would you?"

"Sorry," he said. "My hospitality has certain limits. If I was seen, it would be messy. I make enough trouble for myself without asking for it."

"I wouldn't want you to risk it for nothing," she said. "It would be worth, say . . . a hundred dollars to me."

"A hundred dollars? My God. Listen, if I knew you better, I might chance it for nothing. And then again, I might not."

"I see," she said. "With men it always gets back to that."

"You're wrong there, Valerie. I didn't mean that at all. My wife and I have it good together and she's waiting at home for me right now. I meant, if I understood the situation well enough to know what I might get into."

"That's impossible," she said. "But I'll make it five hundred."

"You have that kind of money!"

"Yes."

There was a time when he could walk away from five hundred without batting an eye if it pleased him. But now it would be exactly five weeks pay, forgetting taxes.

"I could use it," he said. "But I wouldn't take that much from you."

"Don't be foolish," she said. "It wouldn't mean a thing to me. I can afford it."

"Cash?"

"Cash. On delivery."

"No advance?"

"No advance."

"All right. Is there just the one bag?"

"Just one. A tan suitcase. Quite big, but not heavy."

"Wait here," he said. "I'll at least give it a try."

Up on the road a wrecker had arrived. Presently the crew were working at righting the Olds. The activity had drawn the attention of the crowd. But two men in coveralls were examining the Cadillac. A bald, beefy man lifted the hood. "Wonder if she'll start," he said. "Looks okay."

"Thing like this, you never can tell," said the other. "No keys in it anyway. Police must have taken them. Wonder who owns it. Rich sonofabitch."

"Six, seven thousand bucks worth of stuff here," said the beefy one. "Least, there was." He closed the hood and both men walked around the car. They seemed in no hurry to leave. But now the Olds had been hoisted back on its four wheels and the crowd was gaping inside. It gave Daniels an idea.

He made his voice excited. "Say," he said to the men, "looks like they might have found someone else in that Olds, way they're gathered around."

"Yeah?" said the bald one incredulously. "C'mon, Charlie, let's have a look!" They departed at a brisk walk.

The round key was already between thumb and forefinger. Quickly he bent over the rear deck and turned it in the lock. The lid gave and he pulled it up. Spare tire, tools . . . a tan case. He grabbed it. It was somewhat heavier than she had led him to believe. He swung it out and closed the lid. He began to walk away with it, planning to cut through the trees and brush, taking short-cut and concealment. But just as he came around to the front of the car, the beam of a light caught him from behind. He turned.

Flash in hand, an officer was moving towards him on an oblique path from the highway. Fortunately he was separated from the officer by the hood of the car and only his back was visible. Without bending, he let the bag drop from his hand. He kicked it flat, then gave it a frantic shove so that it was partly hidden under the car. He continued on around the convertible, employing a casual attitude of inspection.

The officer came up to him. He wore sergeant's stripes. "We've been looking for you, mister," he said.

"For me?"

"Your car, ain't it?"

"No sir, not mine."

"Then what were you doing with your head in that trunk?"

"Oh . . . see what you mean." His mind raced. "Well . . . I just gave the handle a pull and the lid came up. So I had a look."

The sergeant flashed his light over the ground in the area of the convertible. He barely missed the corner of the suitcase extending near the right front wheel. "I could swear you took something out of that trunk, he said. "Guess you better come along with me, fella. I think this is your wagon."

"I own a '56 Ford parked over on that side road," said Daniels. He fumbled for his wallet and removed the registration. "Here," he said. "This proves it."

The sergeant studied the paper under the flash. He handed it back. "Guess you're okay," he said. "But whoever owns this baby did a quick fade. Mighty quick. Because two of my boys came by just after it happened. Ran right down here and this one was empty. Guy took the keys and beat it."

"Damn strange," said Daniels."

"We'll get him," said the sergeant. "Even if the other joe don't conk out, he'll be in plenty of trouble—leaving the scene of an accident. Likely he caused it."

"Sure," said Daniels. "Guess that's why he ran."

"They never learn," said the sergeant. "Well, goodnight, sir." He went off towards the Olds.

Daniels got his hands on the bag again and this time he slid into the trees without being challenged.

THREE

TEN MILES AND ten minutes later she said, "It sounds like you had a very close call with that sergeant. I don't know how to thank you. Yes I do. With that five hundred dollars. First I want to have a look at the suitcase."

"Don't you trust me?"

"Don't be silly. Of course. But naturally I'm concerned about my things."

"Hold the wheel a minute," he said. "I'll reach back and get it for you."

"Never mind," she said. "One accident is enough."

Before he could protest, she climbed over the seat. With a pretense of looking straight ahead disinterestedly, he flicked his eyes to the rearview mirror. He could see only her head, bent low and away from him. With a deft movement, he gave the mirror a quick down-twist. Now he could see, though vaguely.

She had the lid of the case open. He couldn't make out the contents. She was groping around. Her head turned once to check him. He held his position and she returned her attention to the case. He still couldn't see. But then a car passed from the other direction and for a moment, light flared over the back seat.

She had a stack of bills in her hand, straining to see and count. But this was small change. She was right when she said she could afford the five hundred. The case beneath her hand was crammed to overflowing with a sea of green bills. For all its width and depth, it contained nothing else but money.

Daniels couldn't take his eyes from the mirror. When he did look down, the car was veering across the road. He had to resist the temptation to yank the wheel and give himself away. For the next few moments he raced around in mental circles of useless speculation. As he watched her close

17

the case and swing agilely back to her seat, he thought—
*Just because it's an ocean of money in a suitcase, why does
it HAVE to be suspicious? There could be a dozen ex-
planations. But, my God, so much money! How much . . .?*

She opened the alligator purse and made a show of counting out the bills which she had placed there seconds before.
"Five hundred," she said, and passed him the money.

With only a glance, he put the bills in his pocket.
"Thanks," he said. "And believe me, I earned it. Your clothes
all in order?"

"Uh-huh. Fine."

"Why don't you tell me about it, Valerie? Leave out names
and specific details, if you like. Just the general problem. I
might be able to help."

"No thanks. Everything will be all right—now."

"Not exactly," he said. "They'll check the registration of
that Cadillac back to your friend. Then they'll come looking
for him. But let's say he's moved. They still know who he
is and they will have impounded a very expensive automobile. It doesn't make sense."

"It does if you know the car was rented."

"In that case, don't you care what happened to your
friend?"

"I imagine I'll know where to find him. And that's absolutely all you'll get out of me."

"Okay, Valerie. Sorry you won't let me help beyond the
call of that five hundred. So now you're on your own."

Five hundred bucks. A windfall that would pay his expenses to New York and still leave better than three hundred. Myra would explode with joy. Though perhaps her
joy would be a little dimmed by the complex manner in
which he came by the money. In truth, he wished he had
not seen the contents of the suitcase. For what might have
been only a strange and exciting adventure in which he was
paid handsomely for his daring, had become something a
little soiled with doubt and suspicion. In the back of his
mind there was even a nudge of guilt. He should know the
source of that money. But since the money was dumb and

Valerie resisted examination, there was nothing gained in punishing himself with worry. He would think about it another time—when there was no chance of his doing anything so foolishly righteous as giving it back.

He had called Myra early that morning. It had been a brief conversation. He had not told her the details—only that nothing tangible had worked out. There was no point in spending the money to relate a complete sob story long distance. Myra would only brood and her office-girl day would be spoiled. He left her with the feeling that there was at least some small hope. But was there, really? All the faces he had looked into had been smiling with cold eyes. He did not see in them the smallest wedge of re-entry to his former world of television announcing where the camera-eye revealed him to fifty or more million people a week. And his tax deductions alone had once been five times his present salary.

They rode mostly in silence. Occasionally he asked her a carefully calculated question. But her answers were just as carefully evasive.

They reached the northern outskirts of Miami. He swung over to Biscayne Boulevard. Traffic was sparse on the broad boulevard in the first hour of the morning. He was tired. But his weariness was overcome by a latent excitement.

"What part of town, Valerie? I could drop you."

"Thanks anyway. Just go down Biscayne to the center. At one of the hotels there should be a taxi."

"This time of night, why don't you let me take you?" he urged. No gallantry now. It seemed important and even necessary to know where she lived. "If you live on this side, there's no point driving all the way in."

"I don't."

"The beach, then?"

"No."

"South?"

"No."

"I go West, myself."

"A taxi goes in any direction and I'm in no hurry." She

sat deep in her seat, arms folded, eyes ahead. She sounded cool and withdrawn. For all her crispness, there was about her a lost quality. Yet nothing even vaguely suggestive of the criminal mentality. Absurd. No, not absurd.

In ten minutes he had paused at the curb on a side street before the entrance to one of the big hotels which peered across the bay to the commercial opulence of Miami Beach. A taxi waited just beyond.

For a moment, while he had his hand on the grip of the bag to unload it, he thought of accusing her openly—*Valerie, I saw what you have in this suitcase. You must admit the whole business has a bad smell. Now, either you give me an extremely plausible explanation, or we drive to the nearest police station.*

It sounded corny and over-dramatic when he played it back. There was no law against carrying large sums of money. And further, though innocent, he had been a kind of accomplice after the fact. Especially when he accepted that five hundred he needed so badly. So he swung the bag to the walk while her eyes followed his every movement. He knew she would gladly have made the exertion herself if it would not seem odd.

The cabby opened her door, then hoisted the bag in front with him. Watching her pretty face, Daniels could almost hear her cry of protest.

"Well, thank you," she said quickly. "Thank you—for everything."

"Everything was well paid for. Sure it won't leave you short?" He almost smiled.

"Not at all." Her eyes begged him to hurry.

"I don't even know your full name."

"Millions of people don't and they get along."

"Will I see you again?"

"I think, never. Now, please! I'm so terribly tired."

"Goodnight then, Valerie."

"Goodbye." She watched him coldly.

He stepped back a pace, gave her a small salute and waited. That didn't work either because she merely turned and said, "Straight ahead, driver. I'll tell you." The cab moved off. She didn't look back.

Watching the tail light slowly recede, he had the most dreadful sense of loss. Not of her in any personal sense, naturally. But of something which might connect with her that had been welling up in his mind, only to fall back again into the abyss of memory.

Then, as the taxi cornered north a block away, he caught the memory by the tail and heaved it up for inspection. Again he was driving crosstown in the jigsaw of Manhattan traffic. Half listening to a newscast which contained a terse item datelined—Miami. It was a rather uninformative follow-up on a story which three days ago should have earned headlines. Three days ago he was on the road north. Not listening to the radio, not reading newspapers, but thinking, thinking. Here in New York, lost more than ever in the depressing labyrinth of his own problems, the item called from him only a fleeting observation—that if he was at home and on the meager staff announcing job at the radio-TV station from which he had been vacationed, the story might come to him as a special assignment. At least an interview with certain officials. The thought was gone as he flipped the dial for music.

Now—now of all times, as the taxi disappeared, the item came flashing back, grew into banner headlines. The connection was fantastically remote. And yet . . .

The squeal of his tires jarred the silence and was echoed back in the empty street. The gaping features of a startled doorman flashed into limbo. The corner rushed to meet him. He turned it sharply.

His thought process had not been involved. The caption recalled, the possible association made, then the leap for the car. Consequently, the time gap had been minor. Thus he had been able to gain enough ground to see the cab swing right again, towards Biscayne. He was faintly surprised when, at the intersection, it turned north along the boulevard, in the very direction from which they had come. Still, it seemed characteristic. She would let him take her right past her door and on into town if it served her purpose.

He kept his distance. Always a block or more. He let traffic interpose and cover him. It was not a difficult thing to do. With its lighted dome to advertise itself, the cab was easy to identify. His own car was an inconspicuous gray sedan.

He followed past the docks along the bay, the MacArthur Causeway to the beach, the darkened glass facade of Marsh's Department Store. Back over the identical route. Another mile and the taxi wheeled east towards the bay.

He took his time. If they went down that street it must be her street. And if so, there would be only a few blocks and a dead-end at the water. He didn't make the turn. Too obvious. He paused to look, lights out. The cab was halted somewhere in the middle of the second block. That presented a small problem. He didn't dare follow—not yet. And it was impossible to distinguish precisely which house or apartment building.

He watched. The cab nosed into a drive, backed, and returned towards him. He pulled to the curb. Then when the taxi was forced to wait at the stop sign, he jumped out and ran over.

"Say, driver," he said. "You remember me. I delivered the lady to your cab. She left something in my car. I've only been here once and I can't remember the street number. Can you give it to me?"

The driver stared at him with a look of secret amusement. "She din't gimme no number, buddy. She just says 'Stop here.' So I stop. Big white stucco. A double header with one of them fancy iron lamps out front. Right side. Can't miss it."

"Thanks," said Daniels. And gave him the dollar he had been twisting noticeably on his finger.

"Funny thing," said the driver, pocketing the bill and shoving in gear. "That place is all shuttered up. You know—them hurricane shutters. When you find out how they breathe in there, let me know." He snickered. "S'long, buddy." He gunned off.

Headlights on, Daniels sped down the street, found the white stucco with the wrought iron lamp and braked. No doubt about it, the eyes of the two-story house were sealed over with broad, firm expanses of aluminum panels, the usual measure taken by winter residents who had gone north for the summer. It was hurricane protection which left the house without a livable degree of light or air.

Nevertheless, he got out and made a circle of the premises. No sneaky light glowing from beneath shutters anywhere. Front and back doors panel-sealed. No guest cottage at the rear. No garage apartment.

No Valerie.

Either she had known that he was following or she had acted on a hunch. Once the cab had departed, she must have gone off on foot, carrying an inestimable amount of money. Thousands. Hundreds of thousands? A half million?

Yet, why did she choose this location as a dodge? Unless it was familiar. Walking with a heavy suitcase, she had to live close by. So, clever as she was, she was not infallible. A careful check of the surrounding area might turn up some clue. She had one big strike against her. She was markedly attractive. Pretty girls are often remembered by not-so-pretty neighbors. And what man would forget her?

In spite of these deductions, Daniels was unhappy as he drove away. If he had remembered the newspaper item and connected it a minute earlier, a fortune in rewards for information leading to the arrest and conviction of . . . persons unknown . . . might be his. If he found Valerie again, it would be an exhausting, plodding task. But now he was more determined than ever. A voice whispered that his intuition was correct. And if tomorrow he had to canvass every house and apartment building in a radius of a half mile, he would find her.

At this moment, Valerie was in the phone booth of a bar three blocks away. She had known that the man who called himself Scott Daniels was growing suspicious. He asked too many questions. He wasn't on the make, either. It was something else. She shouldn't have offered him so much money. Yet she had to get results and the five hundred was an irresistible offer. She couldn't risk getting the bag herself. Her sad tale, though not without a grain of truth, might have sounded a little phony to him. But she couldn't think of a better one. That was nothing, however. If he knew what was in the suitcase . . . Even so, he acted strangely.

During the drive in the cab, she had held her vanity mirror handy. She kept watching to see if he followed as she powdered her nose and pretended to inspect herself. She couldn't tell. The cars behind were many and so anonymous. Certainly, if he followed, he must be far back.

But as Clay, once said—'Never take chances. Never assume that you have covered yourself. In any questionable situation, act as though you are in serious danger of discovery and only the cleverest maneuvering will save you.' So she had ordered the driver to proceed north along Biscayne until she told him to turn. That way she could watch awhile to be certain. And when she instructed him to go right at that random street and stop at that random house, it had been just another step in obedience to caution.

Immediately after the cab had gone, she had cut through the backyard of the house, across the adjoining property to the next street and on up to the first corner. Then she had walked south two more blocks and west almost to Biscayne. She was now at the point where from the cab she had spied the bar.

All the way the suitcase had been growing heavier. But what a beautiful, beautiful heaviness. Actually, a whole lifetime of lightness.

The bar had an entrance on the side street and she had slipped quickly inside. Finding the phone booth at the far end of the dim interior, she had consulted the directory. Leaving the door open and squeezing the case partway inside where it touched reassuringly against her, she placed the coin and dialed.

Now she gave her location and told the voice to send a

taxi in all possible haste to the side street door. She would be watching.

They must have radioed a cab floating not far away, for it was there in only a few minutes. She took the bag with her in the back seat and this time gave the driver a specific address.

In less than ten minutes they were cruising the MacArthur Causeway towards the beach and she was looking over her shoulder across the bay at the sweetly blazing skyline of Miami, calm in the certainty that she wasn't followed.

They did not pursue the Causeway to the beach, but turned off where there was a narrow bridge which led to an island. On this island were many beautiful homes along several curving streets. The driver selected one and tooled the cab almost to its end. He paused before one of the least pretentious of the houses, a modern ranch-house design of beige stucco and redwood trim in complete darkness. She paid the driver and refused his offer of help with the bag.

She went around the side and got the key from where it was wedged behind the gas meter. Then she returned to the front door. She was groping for the lock when the door opened swiftly. She went rigid with shock, then exhaled sharply.

"Clay!" she sobbed. "I didn't think you'd be back so soon. Thank God. Oh, thank God!"

FOUR

HE TOOK THE BAG and pulled her inside, shutting the door. The curtains were already drawn. He lighted a single lamp and turned. He was a tall man in his late thirties, broad shouldered, hard of muscle. He had dark red hair gone a little gray at the sides. Except for a nose which was slightly aquiline, his tanned features were strongly attractive. He wore slacks and a madras sport shirt. A small bandage was taped over his left temple. There was about him an air of refinement and command.

Neither spoke. With a look of complete astonishment, he glanced from Valerie to the suitcase. She rushed towards him and they embraced. As he kissed her, he let one big hand follow the heaving curve of her breast beneath the green silk. He undid two buttons of the blouse, kissed her neck and shoulder, the top swell of her breasts. Again he kissed her mouth, then pushed her away gently.

"You got the money!" he said.

She smiled.

"My God, what a woman! How did you ever do it?"

"When you didn't come, I guessed what happened." She sank into a chair and lighted a cigarette with a trembling hand. "Only I thought it was worse for you. I begged a ride from a man. We stopped at the wreck and I sent him to find out. The convertible was there but you were gone. You said you were going to transfer the suitcase to the trunk of the Cadillac and drive off before anyone came. Since you were able to walk away from the crash, I assumed that you had the money and that either you had gone off with it on foot, or it was in the trunk of the Cadillac. It seemed stupid not to know for sure. So I gave this fellow my keys and sent him to open the trunk. I had to make it worth his while. There's more to it. But the important thing is that you're all right, darling. You're safe and you're all right! Aren't you?"

"I'm all right, yes. At least I am now." He paced the room. "It just didn't go the way we planned. After I left you, I drove until I spotted Marty coming the other way in the Olds, about two miles south of where we went off the road. I let him get out of sight in my mirror, then swung around and caught up. I pretended to be passing. I was counting on surprise—cut in and shove him off the road into a crackup, cut out again fast and stop. But I cut too sharp. I hit him with the right rear fender. Then our bumpers locked and I lost control. But I was set for some such emergency and my

reactions were faster. He got the worst of it. He never knew
who it was or what really happened.

"I went off the shoulder and down into the gully. I
smacked a tree and glanced off. That was when I hit my
head. I blacked out and came to again. Blood was trickling
from my head and pouring from my nose. All over me. I
knew I'd have to hurry. The Olds had turned on its side. I
stumbled over to it. Marty was slumped across the seat. He
looked dead or unconscious. It was a nightmare in that
crazy position, but I got the keys out of the switch and the
bag out of the trunk. I put the keys back. Still no car had
come along.

"The Cadillac was banged up, but looked like it would
run okay. There was room to back around and plough out
of there. I tossed the suitcase in the trunk and tried to start.
She turned over but wouldn't catch. Just wouldn't catch!
I was ready to give up and go off with the suitcase on foot,
when I saw lights on the highway. A patrol car pulled up.
They must have been cruising not too far behind. They threw
a spotlight on the Olds and began to swing towards me. I
took the keys and ducked out the door on the other side. I
crawled off into the trees and watched. Two cops came running down. They split up, each one taking a car. One of
them began flashing his light around for me and I crawled
in deeper.

"Then the mob started to come. And another police car. It
looked hopeless. Not a chance to get the money. Besides, I
was weak and sick and drenched with blood. Dead giveaway
if anyone got a look at me. It was a ridiculous risk to try for
that suitcase.

"There were empty cars down a side road. Some joker in
a Pontiac left his motor running. I stole it. Went back to the
roadhouse, pulled up to the door and looked in. You were
gone. Must have passed you on the way. I beat it just as
some big slob was coming out. I took the coast route and
came home. I was sitting here in the dark, trying to figure
an angle on that suitcase when you came up with it."

"What about the Pontiac?"

"I drove it home, cleaned up and changed my clothes. Then I took it back to town, parked it and taxied out."

"Fingerprints?"

"Gloves. You hear anything about Marty when you were there?"

"Not dead, evidently. But in the hospital. He won't be around for awhile."

"Good! Oh God, Val, what would I do without you? Go pour us one on the rocks and then come and tell me the rest of it."

When she had left the room, he carried the suitcase to a chair and opened it. Slowly, absently, he began to finger the bills.

Scott Daniels wheeled west at 36th Street and pushed for home. The tension and excitement under which he had been operating for so many hours had left him depleted. He was suddenly exhausted and there was in him a sense of complete failure. True, he had the equivalent of five weeks salary. But mentally he had already placed the five hundred in escrow pending proof of its real origin. Valerie wasn't going to that much trouble to conceal herself unless he had been close to some tremendous secret, perhaps the secret between the lines of the newspaper item. Close. But close wasn't good enough. It didn't buy your way out of semi-poverty which was compounded by the fact than once you had enough riches and success to make the present doubly drab in contrast. And the trip to New York had been a bust. A total bust.

Milt Lundberg, in charge of TV productions at the Freeman, Pellett and Weber Agency, had been condescending on the phone. He and Debby Lundberg had been guests at their penthouse in Forest Hills, and the lakeside cottage in the Adirondacks—how many times? But now the bastard was downright patronizing as he spoke from that swivel throne in his office. "Didn't know you were in town, old man. Who you selling for?"

"It's a vacation, Milt. If I had a sponsor, you'd be one

of the first to know it. I'm not selling in this town. That's what I want to see you about."

There was a beat of silence, pregnant with self-protective overtones. "Well now listen, kiddo—no can do today. Meeting with the brass in ten minutes. That'll scuttle the morning. Lunch with some VP's at CBS, two client conferences in the afternoon. That clobbers hell out of the whole day. Might be able to squeeze you in first of next week, though. Tell you what—check with Billie next Monday. You remember Billie, my secretary? Sure you do. Well, check with Billie, Monday AM. She'll set you up with a time. Best I can do, baby. Okay?"

Lundberg had elected not to remember that he had a fine apartment overlooking the East River where "friends" could be invited in the evening.

"Hell no, Milt," said Daniels. "It isn't okay. I won't be in town but two, maybe three days. We'll skip it, Milt. You're busy. I know just how it is."

"Well, now wait a minute, Scott. Just hold on a minute. Can't let you get away, old friend and all . . ." Lundberg saving face while figuring the least. "I'll stay over a few minutes. Invite you for dinner, but we have company. Come by the office at four-thirty sharp. Good enough?"

Then Lundberg in his office, swiveling, doodling with a black and gold pen behind a cloud of cigar smoke. A tall, thin man, pale and parrot-nosed, hair dark and sparse, bushy brows over gray-green eyes of many moods, all of them shrewdly acquisitive in one way or another. Facets of a personality that went all too unnoticed in the mists of approval, in the time of the feast.

"So you've got a good thing cooking there in Miami, eh, Scott? The star rises again—but now in the subtropic heavens."

"Very poetic, Milt."

"My God, I envy you, old man. Christ—if I could ever get out of this empire of soot and garbage, laze around on those clean beaches . . . Rum coolers and palm trees. A very good thing, buddy boy."

"Sure," said Daniels. "A very good thing at a hundred a week."

"Well now, after all. It takes time, you know."

"Yeah. It takes time to build yourself up to a hundred and a quarter, tops. Come on down, Milt. Talk realities. I want out of a nowhere staff announcing job in Miami and back to the big-bundle, free-lance gravy here. It's been a good sin-less year now. That should be long enough for the soap-chip and toothpaste guardians of the air-lanes to forgive and forget."

The pen paused in stroke, was returned to the holder in the onyx base. Lundberg sat back complacently and shook his head. "I'm sorry, Scott. They seldom forgive, and they almost never forget. It's one hell of a big family. But it's a family. And the word travels. They know about you—from here to Podunk and Paducah."

"Crap! Come off it, Milt. That's a generality. Sure, there are some who know . . . or guess. But the majority don't. They knew nothing about me in Miami—except that I was once a big deal. I started clean."

"Then you were lucky. And my best advice is to stay there and build a new reputation."

"I came in here to ask you to give me a crack at some-thing, Milt. Something small to start. You could do it. You could bend the right ears with the right words. 'Scott Daniels is changed, Mr. Dobbs. You wouldn't know him. He downs a very occasional beer. He hasn't had a hard drink in over a year. Still one of the best announcers in the business. Let's give him another whirl.' That's all you'd have to say. What about it, Milt?"

Lundberg swung to the window and back. "I'd like to, Scott. But I can't. They wouldn't hear of it upstairs. I couldn't stick my neck out that far. I sit in this chair. But I'm not fastened to it. See what I mean? If this was penny-ante, it would be different. But we're playing with big money —thousands—millions. One goof and we might lose an account that would wipe out a whole department. I believe in you,

Scott. But that's not enough. Get a staff job on one of the nets here. Ease your way in. Then I'll root for you."

"Fine, Milt. Thanks a lot. You'll root for me when I'm practically home. Thanks a lot. And, of course, you'll pick up the phone and get me that staff job for a start, won't you?"

Lundberg's face closed. "No need for that kind of talk, Scott. I'm sorry. But I didn't lift the bottle to your lips." He looked at his watch. "Got to run, kiddo. Keep in touch. I might hear of something."

And over at the network stations—Carleton Lovelace at NBC: "My God, if we had anything at all, Scott, you wouldn't even have to audition. But unfortunately we're already overstaffed. . . ."

Bill Dickson at CBS: ". . . And I really am sorry we have a tight budget, Scott, because we need a man of your caliber . . . don't doubt for a minute you're on the wagon . . . has no bearing on the situation . . . drop in anytime . . ."

George MacDougal at American: ". . . Of course, there's the vacation relief job. Man we had got is sick and we're on overtime. I might be able to swing it with Hartley on some kind of probationary basis. But it's only good for about three months, fella, and you wouldn't want *that* now, would you?"

There was the small difference in phrasing, but all over town the sum total of the answers was the same—we don't gamble on drunks, reformed or otherwise. Nothing for Scott Daniels.

Not that he had ever been by any stretch of the imagination an alcoholic. He just had a few drinks to "loosen up," before he walked on stage for an important show. And then one time he forgot where to stop and overnight the loosening process had become plain free-wheeling.

Essentially, it was a matter of premature advancement. He had too much talent and too little ego. His self-conception always lagged behind his ability—a dangerous situation in a profession where even an obvious mistake before the millions had to be carried off with such aplomb that the audience applauded the natural and graceful manner in which the performer fell flat on his face.

Beneath the studied glossy front which Daniels had presented to the camera lens, he couldn't overcome a devastating fear that he was being hurled too high, too fast. It was the presence of this fear, not the absence of talent, which had been his undoing.

FIVE

DANIELS PARKED THE car in the lot beside the building. Looking up two stories he could see that there was a light from behind the curtain of their bedroom window. After two AM and Myra still up, waiting. Or asleep with an open book in limp fingers.

The moment he closed the door behind him, he heard the padding of bare feet down the hall. Scampering towards him, wearing one of his pajama tops that came to her knees, how tiny she looked without the lift of her high heels. Her auburn hair bounced along across her shoulders. Typically she had not put it up in the bobby-pinned ugliness which she knew he detested because he told her it made her small gamin face look naked as a light bulb.

"I was getting worried," she said against his shoulder, arms pulling him tight. "You said before midnight and—"

He kissed her gently. "Old faithful, still up," he said. "God, it's good to see you, hon. Sorry, you worried. There were complications and no handy phones. Man, I'm beat! But talkative. Let's get comfortable."

He began to walk with her towards the bedroom. "Where's your suitcase, dear?"

"Damn!" he said. "Left it in the car. Never mind. It's locked away and I'm too tired. Nothing I'll need before morning."

In the bedroom he stripped down to his shorts and lay back against the pillows, smoking with an ashtray on his chest. She sat cross-legged, facing him. Her neat little features were made up with the same precise care she might employ if they were about to set forth for some grand and formal affair. All for him. Even in the absurd pajama tops, she managed to look smart and neat. In spite of the hour, her brown eyes were alert with interest.

"All right," she teased. "What complications? A complicated blonde?"

"No. A complicated brunette."

She laughed.

"You think I'm kidding?"

"Probably. But before you make me too jealous to listen, tell me about New York. What did Milt Lundberg say besides—no?"

"It doesn't seem important, now."

"Please?"

He told her briefly about Lundberg and the others.

"I hate them all," she said.

"Don't bother. In a way, you can't blame them."

"Smug, self-righteous little men."

"Self-protective," he corrected.

She lighted a cigarette and waved off the smoke with a gesture of annoyance. "It isn't as if you were some incurable alcoholic, fresh from an institution. What do they want, signed affidavits? All you did was go off the deep end a few times. In that ulcer contest it could happen to anyone. Oh, I wish you had never accepted that ridiculous quiz show SEVEN COME ELEVEN. Even the name is silly. You had to be loaded to watch it, let alone conduct it. Actually, you almost turned it down."

"Almost," he said. "I had a feeling about it. I knew I wasn't ready. But how do you say *no* to a thousand a week? And especially to that little man inside you who forever after would be whispering that you're a gutless wonder. How do you do that?"

"You don't," she said. "You had to take it." She sighed.

"Poor lamb, you look exhausted. Don't you want to sleep? We can talk in the morning. Nothing seems so grim in sunlight."

"You'll be rushing off to work," he said. "Besides, it won't keep."

"Then I'm going to build a pot of coffee. Be right back. Wait for me, darling."

He smiled. "I love you, baby," he said.

She blew him a kiss. Absently he watched the cute sway of her bottom beneath the trail of his pajama top as she departed for the kitchen.

He looked around the bedroom with its shabby rented furniture. It would have been beter, he thought, if I had turned it down. But how do you say—no. . . ?

At the time the quiz show was offered him he didn't need the extra income. Too quickly, he had traveled the climbing announcer's road from small independent station to network staff, to free-lance, New York. The big-money terminus for television. He had accomplished this in four years when some took ten and most never made it at all. He was more surprised than anyone else at his success, calling it a matter of breaks and timing. He never felt quite seasoned or prepared, always a little afraid of sudden failure.

He had a nice free-lance package going for him. Nothing too tricky or painfully demanding. He had contracts to announce the commercials on two coast-to-coast soap operas, a night-time national newscast and a half-hour suspense drama. In every case he sold different products for the same basic sponsor, an enormous company with many lines. He was answerable to the Freeman, Pellett and Weber Advertising Agency, who serviced the account. Occasionally he did voice tracks for the newsreels. Altogether, in round figures, it was good for a very cozy twelve hundred a week.

Of course, you had to have a good voice and a pleasant selling personality. And, you had to understand timing and stage business, exhibiting the product with poise and naturalness. But in the main, it was a matter of reading someone else's script from a teleprompter in such a deceptive way that it appeared to come right from the old heart. It was tense, but not overwhelming. And he would have been content to leave the status in quo indefinitely.

But, no. The sponsor thought he was great and had sales figures to prove it. For all practical purposes, Leeland Dobbs, the executive vice president, was the sponsor. And like most sponsors, Dobbs didn't understand the tremendous difference between reading from a teleprompter and conducting the intricate proceedings of a national quiz show. This required a skilled master of ceremonies who could gracefully ad lib his way through the snarl of contestants, juggle questions, make decisions, be passably amusing, buttress commercials with a few well chosen words of his own . . . and give the impression he was having one hell of a good time doing it.

But Daniels knew the difference. And he was plain scared when Dobbs insisted he wouldn't have anyone else for the new SEVEN COME ELEVEN quiz but Scott Daniels. At a small station he might stumble through, relaxed enough to come up smelling pretty. But with a nationwide show involving a mint of money, there were grave doubts.

He wouldn't forget that opening night. It was a masterpiece of confusion. In rehearsal, Burt Masters, the director, a sour-faced, cold-eyed bastard, had been riding him mercilessly. From the beginning, Masters had wanted in for his own boy, Dick Hurley. Rumor had it that Hurley kicked back part of his fees on the shows Masters got him. In any case, Masters seemed out to destroy his composure.

At airtime he stood tense, uncomfortably rigid in the hot glare. The red lights winked on beneath the camera. The muscles of his face felt wooden, lips formed into a frozen smile. He looked into the lens and saw . . . not the millions of viewers, not the giant shadow of the audience beyond the lights, not from eye-corner the busyness of technicians and floormen, but the sullen contemptuous features of Burt Masters.

Just for a second the image hung there. And then he heard his own voice, saying none of the things he had carefully planned—but strange, inverted sentences, awkwardly composed.

From the lead-in forward, it was bedlam. Most of the contestants were dull and he had to carry them. Yet, one woman talked too much and he couldn't silence her gracefully, though the show was running long. Meanwhile everything he said came back to him stilted, self-conscious. Who was it quipped, 'The best ad-libs are written'? Where were the casual lines of the teleprompter?

Somehow, in the control room where the offender (probably Masters) was never visual, the sequence of the action became confused. They tossed him an early cue for the commercial, he gave the introduction, and then the girl who was to play housewife was offstage. The camera came back to him and he had to stall for an eon of time until she was ready. Then, for some unimaginable reason, the electronic score computer failed to totalize and for a span he had to do sums in his head when his brain was already crowded with a dozen other details.

Everything went wrong.

And, though most of it could be blamed on the kinks of a first night, he had failed to turn defeat into a personal victory by the casual remark, the apt and humorous phrase.

After the show, ringing wet to his socks, he was cornered by Masters. "My God, Daniels, what hayseed windmill station did you blow in from? You want us to write the whole thing out on an idiot board six-feet high? You couldn't talk your way out of a parking ticket if you owned the street. Jesus, you're about as casual as rigor mortis on ice. That was the worst God-awful mess I've witnessed in years. But don't worry about it, lover. I have a sneaking suspicion someone's on the phone right now asking for a new boy."

Daniels almost hit him. Instead he said, "Why don't you recommend Dick Hurley?" and walked away.

The funny thing was that he met Hurley at Schraffts the next day. And Hurley said with a perfectly bland face, "Caught your show last night, Daniels."

"Well?"

"Don't take it too hard. All your luck was stacked the wrong way."

Hurley giving his sincere commercial while placing you off-guard for the kill. But he had a lot of experience as MC.

"How would you have handled it, Dick?"

"Just relax and kid hell out of it. Turn it into a comedy skit. Frankly, you were a little stiff. You had me sweating. You need a couple more shows behind you. Sometimes I belt two or three down before I go on. It helps. Try it. Loosen you up."

"Thanks. I might do that. If I'm not watching at home."

But Lundberg said that while Dobbs was disappointed, he had faith that next week Daniels would improve.

An hour before show time he was falling apart. He had three straight shots and couldn't feel anything but a flush, creeping like fever to his face. However, he did somewhat better. And at least there was variety. Different things went wrong.

The third week he drank manhattans in th bar downstairs. A half dozen. His reactions were slow, his thinking a little vague. A few things got fouled up. But beautifully, he didn't care. He was tempted to snicker right out loud. Once he did.

Lundberg said, "You're going to the other extreme, Scott. You're not easy, you're almost limp. Tighten up. Make it brighter!"

Now the strain was showing in between. He had lost confidence and began to take a few shots before his less demanding shows. Sometimes he slurred his words. Once he lost a whole paragraph. Directorial eyes grew thoughful under creased brows. He was getting the silent treatment at F. P. & W. Lundberg came right out with it: "What's wrong with you lately, buddy boy? Sick? Need a vacation?"

The fourth week of SEVEN COME ELEVEN, he was drunk. Not falling down, but giddy-minded, body-floating drunk. He concealed it to airtime with a superhuman effort. He opened the show with a frenzied burlesque of an MC on fire with enthusiasm. He hurried everything along at a militant, comically fast pace. He was having a wonderful time.

Then suddenly he ran out of gas and when his cue came to lead into the ad-lib close and sponsor plug, he stood loose-jawed and wordless before a live camera coast to coast. He had nearly two minutes to fill and all he could do was stand there and wave, saying over and over, "G'night, g'night, g'night all."

They had to cover with reams of music, shots of the audience, and the word-stretching of the booth announcer. Meanwhile, he had stumbled off stage and collapsed cold in the wings.

Except for a few professionals, the watching world never really caught on. But he was finished. Masters saw to that. Gone also were his other shows, for the same angry sponsor controlled them all.

Within three days most everyone in that tight little unforgiving world knew. All the unseen doors of re-entry were closed. For awhile he did nothing but live up to his reputation. Once an insurance salesman who came to the apartment asked him conversationally what he did for a living.

"I drink," he said. "Now get out and let me go back to work."

When most of the small capital he had put away was gone and there was no income other than the rental of the lakeside cottage, he answered an ad in a trade publication:

OPENING FOR HIGHLY EXPERIENCED AN-NOUNCER IN TOP FLORIDA MARKET. FORTY HOUR WEEK. $90. EXCELLENT FUTURE. SEND TAPE, PHOTO AND BACKGROUND. REFERENCES REQUIRED.

There was a box number, care of the publication.

Lundberg gave him a reference with his usual condescension. He didn't need it. He was well known. Fortunately, the reason for his disappearance from the monitor screens in their control room was a mystery to the Miami station. He supplied a reason of his own—temporary loss of health with the present need of a new climate. They were glad to get him. In time he got a ten dollar raise—a very big deal. Except for an occasional beer, he had lived in total abstinence.

And through it all Myra reasoned, comforted, adjusted downward without complaint, and took a secretarial job. No wonder theirs had become an inviolate closeness.

She entered now with coffee and cinnamon toast on a tray. "You look terribly thoughtful," she said as he munched and sipped in silence.

Again he glanced around the bleak, heat-soggy room. He was struck by a sickening wave of depression. "Myra, baby. What happened to it all? Gone. Gone."

She reached over and stroked his head. "It's not so terribly important, darling. I don't mind. I mean it. In a different way, haven't we been just as happy? What's gone? Pressures? The mad chase? Cocktail parties? Our fair-weather, politic friends? We've had time for each other. And there's a certain crazy laughable unity in just making do. We talk for hours and we read books and go to movies and take walks. So don't be sad, sweetheart. What's gone that we can't really do without?"

"My face is gone from better than fifty million screens a week," he said. "Money gone, the big car, furniture, clothes . . . and the feeling that I'm not a failure. That's what's gone." He wanted to cry. "But, baby, you're not gone. Stick around, will you? Like forever."

She kissed him. "Like forever." She smiled. "But not if you can't stay away from complicated brunettes. Was there really a brunette?"

He reached for his trousers across a chair next to the bed. From a pocket he produced the five hundred dollars. "See this?" He held up the roll. "It was given to me by that complicated brunette for services rendered. Five hundred bucks."

"Five hundred!" she said. "That's a lot of service. You're not serious. Are you?"

For the first time he inspected the money closely. "Old bills," he said. "Disappointing."

"Old bills, new bills. What's the difference? It spends."

"You can't trace old bills," he answered thoughtfully.

"Can't trace them? What on earth are you talking about now?"

He gave her an exact accounting of the adventure.

"So what does it all mean?" she said.

"It means that if we can't spend this five hundred now, we might be able to bank fifty thousand later. That would be the aggregate reward from various sources, namely a local newspaper, the bank and the city government. It amounts to about ten percent of the total theft."

"Please, honey, make sense."

He mashed his cigarette, removed the tray and sat up sharply. "While I was gone," he said, "in fact, about the same day I hit the road, don't you remember a very sensational story in the paper concerning an armed robbery with a take of a half million or so?"

She looked at him blankly. Then her eyes widened, her mouth worked. "The Second National Bank!"

"Of course."

"Two men wearing masks," she said quickly. "They held up the chief teller seconds after an armored truck made a payroll transfer from the First National. Perfect timing. The biggest haul since the Brinks robbery."

"Right!" he said. "Anything else?"

"Yes. Someone sounded the alarm," she said excitedly. "There was a squad car just a few blocks away and headquarters flashed it. The police were there in a couple of minutes. Then the whole area was blocked off. They never could figure how the crooks got away. It seemed impossible. Not a trace of them. Not a single clue."

"Exactly," he said.

"And you think the money in that suitcase . . ."

"The odds are good. But so far it's just a hunch."

"And you have a plan?"

"I'm figuring one. And I've got six days' vacation left to work it out."

"Sounds dangerous, darling. Don't take chances. Why

don't you talk to Bill Hoag, that detective? The one who took you out cruising around for that show you did—NIGHT PATROL."

"I will. I will. After I've done most of the groundwork. Bill's a nice guy. But I don't plan on sharing the spoils."

He got up and began to pace slowly.

"You ought to get some sleep, dear."

"I know, I know." He went over to the window and, parting the curtain, peered out.

"It's exciting," she said. "And yet . . . frightening, too. Do you have any idea where you're going to start?"

He looked out upon the low buildings of the littered street, then east to the vast dim radiance of greater Miami.

"I'm going to start," he said, "by looking for a girl somewhere out there, named Valerie."

SIX

ON TUESDAY, LATE the following day, after traveling some one hundred sixty miles, Roy Whalen stormed in from Haines City, Florida, and parked his Plymouth sedan beside the Glades Garage on Highway 27. He climbed out and leaned against the door, puffing a cigarette, glancing around the building with a look of squinting speculation.

He was a medium-sized man of thirty-six, a chunky blond with pale freckled skin and blunt features. There was nothing in the least remarkable about him—unless you noticed his eyes. They were azure, flawless as fine gems—and just as hard.

After a moment he gave the cigarette a high flip and made his way around the building to the lot which adjoined it, an area of tall grass and broken rows of wrecked automobiles. He spotted the cream and red Olds almost immediately. With a furtive gaze towards the garage, and with much indirection, pausing to examine other wrecks, he made his way to it.

Pursing his lips, he inspected the crushed right side, the interior with its bent wheel, blood-stained seat, cracked windshield. Then, casually, he circled to the rear.

The trunk lid looked closed, but on closer observation appeared to be slightly ajar. He squatted down, his head beneath the bumper, making a fake study of the undercarriage. If anyone came along he would say he was a body repair man, searching for a late model Olds he could buy for a song and hammer together in his spare time.

But as he brought his head up, his eyes came level with the opening and he was able to see clearly that the trunk was empty. Thus an entirely different story would be needed.

He went now directly to the garage and located the small cluttered office, inside to the left. Here a grimy, unshaven butterball of a man in his undershirt penciled what looked like someone's bill for services.

He looked up, said, "What's yours, friend?"

"Insurance adjuster. You got that Olds '57 sedan, belonged to Martin Bates?"

"You were looking right at it a minute ago, friend."

Whelan's face didn't alter. "That right? Thought so. But I wasn't sure."

"That's the heap. You got here fast enough. Poor bastard ain't even cold yet. They tell me he kicked off without never comin' to."

"I know. We got it from one of his relatives. That's the way it goes."

"Come up from Miami, friend?"

"Yup. You have the damage estimate?"

With a grunt the man opened a drawer, brought out a sheaf of papers, selected one, handed it over.

"My God," said Whelan, "this is a beaut! I'll take it along if you've got a copy."

"Got two."

"Now," said Whelan, "the brother, Matthew Bates, said

there were some personal effects. Should be a couple of suitcases. Authorized me to pick 'em up."

"Just one suitcase, friend." He pointed. "That's it up there —black one on the shelf. Nothing in it but a few shirts, underwear, stuff like that. I was here when the highway boys had a look at it."

"That's all? No other suitcase? A big tan one?"

"Nope. Cop come in behind the wreck opened the trunk hisself. Just the black one."

"They couldn't have taken the case out at the scene of the accident?"

"Nope. Not hardly. Never do it that way. Bring the heap in first—always."

For the first time, Whalen was hard put to keep his face empty and his voice under control. "Well, Jesus," he said, "that's mighty strange. The brother says the case was there, big tan job. Some clothes in it belonged to him, other stuff worth a few hundred. It couldn't just walk away without a little help. Now if he puts in a claim, we'll have to have a pretty thorough investigation. Tell you what. Just for the hell of it, give the highway patrol a call and see if they know anything about it."

The garage man gave him a look to indicate the insanity of such a proposal, then reached for the phone. After placing the call he was obviously shuffled around until the informed party was reached. He posed the question, listened, made a few grunts into the mouthpiece and hung up.

"Nothing doing," he said. "Cops was there first and that trunk wasn't touched until she was hauled in here."

Whalen looked at the man steadily a moment. Something told him the guy wasn't hiding anything. "What about the other car in the wreck—the Caddy?" he said. "Luggage in that one?"

"You got a claim on both of 'em?"

Whalen shook his head. "Just curious."

"Empty," said the man. "And I mean *empty!*" He leaned forward confidentially. "A real screwy situation. They never did find the character who was drivin' it. Ran off somewhere.

Then they trace the registration and they find it's a stolen car. Unreported. Guy who owns it lives back north. Loaded. He has a bunch of cars. He leaves this one in his own garage over in Miami Beach . . . and someone swipes it. This is the first he hears about it."

Only this last was news to Whalen. He had read the rest in the late morning paper and had set out immediately, first phoning the hospital to make sure there was no mistake about Marty's death.

"Damn queer, all right," he said. "You can bet your tail we'll be looking into it. Well, thanks a lot, fella. You'll hear from us."

"You wanna leave your card just in case we. . . ."

"Nah," Whalen called over his shoulder at the door. "I'll be around. S'long."

He went out quickly and drove off.

As Roy Whalen reached the outskirts of Miami, darkness was settling fast. All the way he had accomplished some serious and much involved thinking. The whole deal had a very bad stink and he was going to follow his nose where it led him. It was too bad about Marty. Really, too bad. Marty had been one of the last remaining people in this world he could trust. And there had been a certain special feeling between himself and Marty Bates. Too bad.

But in all ways, Whalen was a practical man. When a thing was done, it was done. When a man was dead, he was dead. Real dead. His usefulness was over. No point in raging or weeping around. Both made your mind sloppy when there were things to be done.

At a stoplight, Whalen removed the keys from the ignition and opened the glove compartment. From it he took a snub-nosed .38 caliber Smith and Wesson revolver. The gun still felt strange in his hand. Until a week ago when his life had undergone some fantastic changes, he had never before carried such a weapon. Now he dropped the .38 in his pocket, returned the keys to the switch, restarted and boomed away.

He had a sudden vision of Marty standing in the doorway

the night they separated. Marty smiling and saying, "What's the matter, Roy? You look worried. If you think I'll skip, let *me* check the route out and you follow later with the dough. I'd trust you with it anytime."

No, Roy Whalen didn't think Marty Bates had pulled a fast one before he was killed. The disappearance of the person or persons who were in the Cadillac made him believe it happened another way. Another way entirely.

And who else but Clay and Valerie knew anything at all about the money?"

When Clay unlocked the door, Valerie was in the living room pouring martinis into frosted glasses.

"I heard you," she said. "And I knew you'd want one of these."

Her smile was not the broad reckless thing it had once been for him. She was constantly on edge lately. Nevertheless, there was warmth in her eyes and she wore that tight pink sweater and a hip-snug skirt. He felt the instant surge of desire.

He dropped the newspaper on a table and she handed him the glass. He couldn't sip. He had to gulp it down.

"There's no race, darling," she said. "You're awfully late, aren't you?"

"Tough day," he muttered. "I couldn't seem to concentrate on all that routine crap. Pour me another, will you, honey?"

She filled his glass and he walked around aimlessly, wanting to touch her but not yet unwound enough to do even that. As he expected, she picked up the paper and began to study it with frowning attention.

"Third page," he said. "Column four."

She flipped the sheet in a flurry of haste. She found it and for half a minute scanned furiously, biting down on her lip. Then she dropped the paper in a heap and looked up with a broken expression.

"He died," she almost whispered. "He died."

"I admit it's a shock," he said. "But we knew the risk. And there's a certain safety. . . ."

"I just didn't expect him to die," she said in an awed tone. "I thought maybe he would be in the hospital awhile and then. . . . Oh, I don't know what I thought! I wish I had never known Marty, never seen him. It's . . . it's so personal."

"He was nothing to you."

"Well, I know, but after all . . . Clay, what are we coming to? We should get out of here. Now! There are planes that can take you overnight to . . . to anywhere."

"Don't get panicky, Val. Just don't get panicky." He finished the second drink, chewed the olive, sat down and lit a cigarette. "You know very well I can't possibly leave. How would it look?"

"How long, then?"

"I told you. About three months. Sooner if it seems a completely dead issue."

"Three months, three months. It's a lifetime with your nerves just screaming for relief. I won't be able to take it."

"Yes you will."

"I ought not to stay here," she said. "I should move back to the apartment. Suppose I was seen by someone in the neighborhood. They don't know your wife is in Reno getting a divorce. It would cause talk. And one thing might lead to another."

"Just stay hidden, Val honey. That's all."

"I feel like a prisoner. I'm so wretchedly lonely here all day. I want to have fun, Clay. Good times. We have this complete fortune and what good is it? Worthless!"

"You think you wouldn't be more lonely in that apartment? I need you, honey. I need you."

She was silent. Then, "What did you hear about the hold-up? Anything new? They don't suspect a thing?"

"Of course not. They're running around in circles. They can't understand how the—the culprits, as the paper likes to call them, got away. Captain Krause told me he thinks they could have slipped on a plane or a train before the terminal or the depot was put under watch. He's sure they didn't get away by car. All roads were screened tight. It's a joke. What are they going to do without a description—check every human being in transit anywhere? And his luggage? Still, I'm glad we didn't take chances. The best news is that the cops are looking for professional stick-up artists. I was counting on that. It certainly was clever enough for any professional in the country."

"Exceedingly clever, darling. But I'm in no mood to brag—not that one brave idea was mine. I'm thinking about Roy. He reads newspapers like anyone else. By tonight or tomorrow he'll be burning his tires in all directions, asking questions, questions. And if the answers don't make sense to him, he has just one more place to go."

"Roy will be a long time getting around to us," Clay answered. "And if it comes to that, I can handle him with my best astonishment and innocence approach.

"Look at it this way—he has not a thing, not a shred to accuse us with. After we split the cash we were not supposed to have an inkling of their future plans. How could Roy know you were cozy with Marty? You think Marty would have told him? Not on your life. So then, in Roy's little brain there is left the conception that we would not know time, place, or even method of their departure. And further, I don't believe he would even guess that we—that I was the type for such a cross."

"Yes, but he doesn't think like you and I, Clay. No subtle shadings. Don't expect him to figure us incapable of anything just because we make pretty talk and have nice manners."

"And further," continued Clay, "the Cadillac doesn't connect and never will. So he's got to come to one of three conclusions. Either Marty crossed him and hid the money, or it was stolen from the car sometime after the so-called accident. Or again, and finally, the police have it and are keeping their mouths shut while they check it. Satisfied?"

"Almost. I would be if there wasn't a half million, seventeen hundred dollars involved. And if Roy Whalen wasn't about the most determined animal I ever met."

"Even if he guessed," said Clay, "there isn't a chance he'll find it where it's hidden."

She stood and came to him. "Let me look at that gash," she said, leaning over him and tilting his head into the light. "Not bad from any distance at all. The make-up covers it and the swelling's gone down. If you didn't have a good tan you'd be in trouble. Anyone notice it?"

"Not a single mention." Above him, pendulous and swollen, her breasts were a sudden demand for attention. He pulled her down.

"Darling—aren't you hungry? It's going on—"

"Yes, I'm hungry. For you."

He reached under her sweater and with one neat wrench, undid her bra. She looked toward the windows.

"All curtains closed," he said.

"Later, darling?"

"Now!"

"Well then, why do we stay here?"

"I like to progress slowly from chair to couch to bed." He chuckled. "It dates back to my days of fumbling excitement. When it never got to the bed."

She smiled the old reckless smile and pulled the sweater over her head. She sloped her shoulders and slipped out of the bra. "There. Do you like?"

Her breasts were large but compact and insolently uptilted. The areas surrounding her nipples were enormous dark circles, bull's eye caps to the round peaks of flesh.

Fascinated, he stared and stared. Then pulled her against him.

"Make it so we don't think, darling," she murmured. "So we never have to think again."

But later, in the bedroom, when in silence they had both begun to think more clearly than ever, there was the startling sound of someone beating on the front door with increasing tempo and rising impatience.

In the glow from the hall light, they looked at each other. He bounced out of bed and began to pull on trousers and shirt over his nakedness. He slipped bare feet into moccasins, then pulled open the drawer of the night table. From it he took a .45 caliber automatic, flushed a round into the chamber and stuffed the gun into his hip pocket.

"My God, my God," she moaned. "Like a gangster and his moll everytime someone comes to the door."

"Shut up and get dressed," he said. "Hurry! But stay right here. I'll come for you if I want you."

He looked and the butt of the gun was visible. He pulled his suitcoat from the chair and threw it on with his ready mask of dignified annoyance.

Trembling, he went out to the door.

SEVEN

SCOTT AND MYRA Daniels sat in a booth of the little Italian restaurant around the corner from their apartment. Myra took a sip of the port wine while Scott absently twirled spaghetti around his fork.

"Sure—I know it had to be done," he said. "But just the same, I feel like the whole day was wasted. A big zero. I combed that entire vicinity block-by-block. I described that girl like she was my own sister. Exactly two leads, both false. But how could I know they were false? I had to check them out, didn't I? More time shot. And did you ever search an entire phone book for Valeries? Try it sometime." He forked the spaghetti into his mouth.

"Were there many Valeries?" asked Myra.

He swallowed. "A whole bunch of them. But not as many as you might imagine. It's not such a common name. I called every last one of them because I think I might recognize her voice. It's kind of throaty and has a . . . what shall I call it? . . . finishing school quality."

"And what happened?" said Myra.

"Well, it was rather complicated. If a man answered, which wasn't too often, thank God—I had one story. If a woman answered, I had another. Mostly I was very formal and pretended that I had the wrong Valerie Glutz, a person I understood to be in Miami but couldn't locate. It didn't matter what I said once I was sure the voice on the other end was not *the* Valerie. Four Valeries didn't answer, probably because three of them were working girls. I called them again after business hours and got all but one. However, with the chick I couldn't reach, someone did come to the phone to say that Valerie was her mother and was sixty-seven years old. Hardly my girl. Nor were any of the others."

Myra frowned, toyed with her salad. "Don't you think she might have made the name up?"

"Possibly. But my feeling is that she didn't. In the first place, it doesn't seem logical that if you were going to invent a name, one like Valerie would just pop into your head. Jane, Betty, Helen, Joan or Martha, maybe. But not Valerie. And, in the second place, she was terribly distracted. The name slipped out naturally and without hesitation. For the time being, I'm going to assume it wasn't a phony. I have to start somewhere."

"So she just doesn't have a phone," said Myra. "Or it's under her husband's name."

"She wasn't wearing a wedding ring," said Scott. "Proves nothing, really. But I still don't think she was married."

They became busy with their food. Myra was pensive.

"Wasn't it awful that poor man died in the accident," she said.

"Grim. Glad I didn't get there in time for a look at him. Bates—Martin Bates. Paper said he was a watchmaker. Had his own little one-man shop downtown somewhere." Scott picked up the folded paper beside him and ran his finger down a column. "Says here . . . 'He is survived by his brother, Matthew Bates, Springfield, Illinois. An employee of the building which houses the clock shop stated that Bates was enroute to visit his brother. However, reached in Springfield, Matthew Bates expressed surprise at this explanation. Mr. Bates said he was not aware of his brother's intention to visit with him.

" 'A wide search is under way for the missing hit-run

driver of the stolen Cadillac involved in the accident. Theft of the car was not learned until . . .' And so on. I told you about all that."

"Everything connected with the accident is so odd," said Myra. "Of course the driver of the Cadillac ran because he knew they'd catch him with a stolen car."

"To say nothing of a suitcase overloaded with wads of dough, probably just as stolen," added Scott. "But why would a guy with that much cash take a chance on stealing an automobile? And in God's name, where the hell was he going when he got in the wreck? Well, it will all come out in the wash. And that's one bundle I want to wash personally. On top of the money-reward, it seems like something I just *have* to do."

"Please, please be careful," said Myra, touching his hand.

"Oh, I will, hon. If I ever get close enough again to be careful."

"What's the plan for tomorrow, then?"

"Tomorrow I'll go to the Second National Bank. As a reporter type from WKSR-TV, I should be able to wrangle some information on just exactly what happened in the robbery. From there, we'll see. All finished? How about some dessert? We're really splurging tonight."

"No thanks, dear," said Myra. "I can't work up the least enthusiasm about spumoni."

EIGHT

Roy Whalen sat easy in his chair across the living room from Clay. Ever since Clay had opened the door and he strode into the room, Roy had seemed deceptively relaxed, speaking of Marty and the lost money in that breezy and caustic manner which Clay knew was only skin deep. Tension hung around Whalen like gas from a leaking main.

"I dunno," he concluded, "guess I just don't have your

head for figures, Clay boy. It won't add up. I come out minus three hundred seventy-five grand and Marty gets a big zero for keeps."

"Of course I read the newspaper account," said Clay smoothly. "And while to me Marty was strictly a business proposition, I was pretty shaken. To say nothing of the fact that it didn't make sense. What was he doing on Route 27 out in the Everglades and completely alone? I thought you two might still be in town. Or at least that you would take off somewhere together. But then, you never seemed willing to discuss your plans. So how could I understand all this?"

"That's right," said Roy reasonably, nodding his head, pursing his lips. "I remember. We never told you a thing." His eyes in the flat features were a study in crystal-blue innocence. "Not that we didn't trust you, Clay boy. It just seemed like a sharper operation to keep a few items to ourselves. But now that Marty's dead and the cash is . . . nowhere . . . I can't see any harm in giving you the rundown."

"Please do," said Clay. "After all, we've got to stick together. It's a dangerous situation. And maybe I can see some possibilities."

"That's what I like about you executive types," said Whalen. "Real gentlemen. Always ready to help in any little boy-scout emergency."

"Never mind the cute sarcasm, Roy," said Clay in his brass-tacks, right-on-your-level voice. "I know you're bitter about your friend and the money, but—"

"Especially the money—now," said Whalen. "Three hundred seventy-five thousand simoleons—all friends—if I can find them. So we'll can the crap and get down to the meat. Now, here's the way it was set up.

"We had to get rid of our cut. You can't just leave three hundred seventy-five grand sitting around in a suitcase." He smiled slyly. "It might get stolen. So we decided the first thing to do was to get it out of the state where it was hot. Not that they could trace old bills, but they would be watching for any large sums to show. After we got it out of the state, we figured the best place to put it was . . . where? Where else? Banks, of course. Lots and lots of banks.

"So we had it mapped out to cross into the nearest state— Peachy-keenville, USA—Georgia. Then we would haul over to Atlanta, a nice big city. And there we would go down to a half dozen or more of that city's staunchest banks and open accounts, each in his own dreamed-up name. Nothing big, you understand. That would be dangerous. Not a penny over five thousand per account. No raised eyebrows at all.

"But that wouldn't end it. We would hang around for three, four days making deposits on these accounts, up to ten, fifteen grand each bank. It's opening the account you have to be careful. After—who's to question deposits? Some jerk teller? Hell, no. Right, Clay?"

"That's right, Roy." Clay no longer wondered why Whalen bothered to explain the plan. He was proud of it and this was opportunity.

"But still," he continued, "we don't gamble by dropping too many eggs in one basket. So after a few days we move on. To New Orleans. Same thing all over again. Then slowly, we head west, shedding gold all the way. In only the big cities. Finally, we wind up on the coast—like L. A. We drop the rest of the loot, maybe seventy-five grand between us, in banks around town.

"Then we buy some kind of small business we can use as a dodge. For this we have a nice commercial account and very slowly we start pumping money into it from these nest eggs around the country. Neat, Clay?"

"Quite."

"But we have one problem. First we have to get the money out of the state of Florida. And the newspapers, to say nothing of your personal contacts, tell us that trains, planes, ships and all roads are being watched. But how long do they set up roadblocks? A day? Two days? Three? Four at the most. After that, what the hell. . . . So we figure on five. But we have to know. We can't guess. So I agree to go on ahead about half-way across the state on Route 27 to Haines City. If I get through without a whisper, then I phone Marty, tell him it's okay to drive up and bring the cash, meet me at Haines in a certain motel. Also, this way we're not two guys traveling together—just what the boys might be looking for.

"Next day I go on ahead and cross into Georgia. If it's okay, I phone Marty to follow right behind and we meet in Atlanta. We sell one car and shove off again. Don't you think it would have worked, Clay?"

"I think so," he answered. "It was well thought out."

"You think so—and I know so. Now, Clay boy, you just tell me this, what went wrong? Who would have the best chance of crossing us up and grabbing that cash?"

"How should I know!" said Clay sharply, reaching for some offensive position to cover his growing fear that Roy might have a clue. "From your story of the check you made after the accident, it seems to me you've overlooked several possibilities."

"For instance?"

"Why for God's sake, Roy, anything could have happened. You've got people milling all over the place at the wreck. Suppose the force of the crash had snapped that trunk lock open and—"

"Don't hand me that, Clay. You got a lot of people around, one wise-guy won't risk it. He don't even know what he's after. Don't give me that."

"I'm not giving you a goddam thing, Roy. You sound like the prosecuting attorney. I don't have to defend myself. You got more than your share. What you did with it is your business. If you don't want a little friendly advice, don't waste my time. Just get out."

Roy smiled his bored, I'm-waiting smile. "So what else is new, Clay?"

Clay was silent. Might as well play all the cards and see if there was a trump out. If only the accident arrangement had gone as planned. There would have been no second car with a missing driver. Just Marty—careless, sleepy, drunk—but off the road without any apparent help. No questions.

"It never occurred to me that Marty might have the money with him," said Clay. "So I haven't had much time to think about it. But right off the top of the mind, let's see. . . . You said the car was hauled in by a wrecker. A wrecker has a crew. They couldn't have been watched every minute . . . ."

"Anything else, Clay?"

"Well, sure. You can think as well as I can. The cops take the case and put it in one of the patrol cars. Routine. Later, they check it. Right away they guess the money is stolen. One, they keep it. Or two, they hold it for investigation. If so, they're certainly not giving out any information."

"Yeah," said Roy. "But they would lay for some guy like me to come around. If that was the case, I'd be in the pokey right now. It was a chance I had to take. Give me another idea."

"As much as I hate to say this," replied Clay, "did it ever occur to you that Marty could find that much money awfully tempting? He might have disposed of it before the accident."

"It occurred to me," said Roy. "But then I got wondering why he was on the right road, headed in the right direction. See what I mean? Can you think of one more, Clay boy?"

Clay assumed an attitude of deep consideration. "On short notice," he said finally, "that's as far as I can go with it."

Roy shifted in his chair, lighted a cigarette, exhaled luxuriously. "You know," he said, "it kind of disappoints me that a brain like you could miss one big angle. It's a real surprise to me that an ignorant, stumble-along cluck like me could out-reason you. I'm too modest to believe it possible."

"Cut it, Roy. I'm already impressed."

"So now tell me, Clay. How could you forget about the driver of the Caddy? Huh? If the bastard could swipe a car, he could swipe cash, couldn't he? And then beat it—fast."

"I didn't overlook that," said Clay quickly. "I passed over it because it didn't make sense. Even if he had time for all that, and wasn't hurt so badly he could just about crawl away, he wouldn't stop to search for money he didn't know existed."

"Ahhh," said Roy, "that's the rub. But suppose he *did* know it existed."

Clay swallowed. "How?"

Roy got up and walked over to stand before Clay's chair. All expression had left his face. "I'll tell you how. You told him, pal. You told him."

"What? Nonsense!"

"That's it, you told him. You got hold of some punk for a few grand and you tipped him to follow Marty. He grabbed the case and brought it to you."

"Ridiculous! How could I tell him to follow Marty if I didn't know the first thing about your plan?"

"I haven't figured that one yet. But I don't need it. Because I can tell by looking at you I'm goddam close. When I came over here, I was in the dark. Just groping around for any kind of an answer, listening to a hunch. But when a guy like you forgets to mention some obvious angle like what gives with the missing stooge in the Caddy, it must be because he's got something to hide. Where's the money, Clay?"

"Don't try to start anything with me, Roy. You'll come out on the wrong end."

"You scare me. Where's that dough!"

"Get out, Roy. For the last time, get out."

Roy ignored him and began to walk around, opening a closet, studying the room. "Of course," he said, "knowing you, it's probably so well hidden I'll have to beat your head open to find it. But I'll just go through the motions first." He went towards one of the bedrooms—the wrong one.

"Whalen! I wouldn't go in there. I've got company." Clay stood and let his hand rest behind him on the butt of the .45 beneath his coat.

Roy turned. "Don't tell me," he said. "Let me guess. Come on out, Valerie!" he called.

Valerie opened the door and walked into the room. Again she was wearing the tight skirt and pink sweater. In fear

and haste she had obviously pulled the sweater over nakedness.

With his eyes, Roy very carefully removed the sweater,
then the skirt. He seemed to store the picture away before
his gaze came up to her face. "Hello, Val. How's it go? Getting your kicks?"

Valerie gave him a look of icy disdain. But he stared her
down and she walked away, settling into the chair by which
Clay was standing.

"What a cozy little nest," said Roy. "All the luxuries. You
have expensive taste, Clay. I've always wished I could afford
a gal like Valerie. But I never had the money. Let's see if
we can't find just what it is that holds her interest—aside
from your own personal magnetism, of course." Again he
walked towards the bedroom.

"Don't bother, Roy. You're leaving."

It was said with such calm conviction that Roy paused to
look over his shoulder into the wide mouth of the gun. He
came back a ways, but did not seem frightened.

"Expecting trouble, Clay? You don't seem the type to
carry a gun."

"My character changes with circumstances," said Clay. "I
adapt quickly. But just for your peace of mind—you wouldn't
have found what you came for. We don't have it and never
did."

Roy scratched his nose with an index finger. "Well now,
it seems to me that with a big .45 in your hand you're a
little too anxious to convince me."

"Goodbye, Roy. And I mean *goodbye*."

Whalen went to the door and turned. "Of course you
haven't got the guts," he said. "But you'd be a lot safer if
you just pulled that trigger right now, Clay. I never saw the
inside of a jail, but I risked a long stretch to get that money.
I gambled my whole life on it. Marty Bates died for his
share which I now consider to be mine. And as far as I'm
concerned, without that three hundred seventy-five thousand,
I'm just as good as dead. I'll be a dead man walking around
looking for his life-blood. Twenty-four hours a day, awake or

asleep, I'll be scheming ways to beat you, Clay—if I have to kill you to do it. Wherever you go, whatever you do, just keep thinking about that. Enjoy yourself, buddy boy. S'long."

They looked at each other.

He went out the door.

"My God, he means it," said Valerie in a husky voice. "He means every word. Clay, I'm scared. What are we going to do? What can we possibly do now. . . ?"

NINE

THE HEAD TELLER of the Second National Bank in the Commercial Exchange Building on Flagler Street, was a small thin man with a narrow face, a wiry mop of gray hair and placid gray eyes behind steel-rimmed glasses.

"I thought you looked familiar, Mr. Daniels," he said leaning forward from his window. "And now that you mention WKSR, it comes back to me right away. The wife and I used to watch you on that NIGHT PATROL program. Interesting show. Yes, indeed. Well, sir, what can I do for you?"

"The station," said Scott, "is considering a new program called CLASSIC CRIMES, UNSOLVED. It would be a series of interviews with police officials and laymen having knowledge of any of the more spectacular crimes which have gone unsolved. Aside from its news and entertainment value, we would hope to enlist the aid of the public in furnishing clues which previously might have been thought unimportant. The police would bring to light some of the lesser known facts of the case and this in turn might stir the public memory. There are all kinds of possibilities. And, for a starter, I've been assigned to investigate the details surrounding the robbery of this bank."

Actually, Scott had dreamed up the idea the night before as a gimmick to get information, only to find that it was surprisingly sound. Clint Rolley, the Program Director, was dubious but could see no harm in giving sanction if Daniels was willing to expend his own time gathering material for a pilot show.

"Well," said the head teller, whose name was Wilkins, "you can count on me for full cooperation. Anything that would help to bring those men to—"

"Thank you," said Scott. "Now, what time did the robbery occur?"

"It was just about ten minutes before ten on a Thursday morning, the 29th. We opened as usual at 9:30."

Scott smiled. "You wouldn't forget that, would you?"

Wilkins gave his head a vigorous shake. "Never. We had to meet several payrolls on the following day. Firms in this building and others in the neighborhood that issue their paychecks on the fifteenth and thirtieth of the month. An accumulation of two-weeks' pay per employee can add up to a lot of money. The cash had to be counted on Thursday and dispersed on Friday."

"Now where did this money come from, Mr. Wilkins?"

"Depends on how far you want to go back. Originally it came with a larger amount from the nearest Federal Reserve Bank in Jacksonville. Brinks handled the delivery to the First National."

"A branch of this bank?"

"No, sir. There are no branch banks in Florida by state law. But First National has the largest amount of cash on hand in the city and smaller banks like this one have accounts there. When we need extra cash to meet large payrolls, we draw it from them. As in this case, the money is delivered by a local armored trucking outfit."

"All right," said Scott. "Now we know where it came from and for what purpose. But the robbery took place after the money was delivered. Right?"

"That's right. Within a minute or two. I was just getting ready to transfer it to the vault until we were ready to count it."

"And what happened?"

"Well, it seemed like the guards had hardly gone out the door when I found myself looking into the barrel of a revolver. There were two men, both wearing white coveralls —the kind painters use. They wore white gloves and those peaked painters' caps. One of them even had a paint brush tucked in his belt."

"And masks?"

"Yes, of a sort. Black strips of cloth which hung down from under their caps, covering their faces and leaving slits for the eyes."

"Strange get-up," said Scott. "You could tell nothing about them?"

"Nothing worthwhile. Two men, hard-voiced but not particularly—you know, ungrammatical in their speech. One was taller than the other. I can't tell you another thing. You couldn't see much of their builds in those loose coveralls."

"Just what did they do and say?"

"I didn't see them approach," said Wilkins. "I was bent over the sacks. I felt the presence of someone at the window and looked up into the gun.

" 'It's not your money, bud,' this voice said. 'So don't take a chance on a slug through your brain. Press the little button and let my friend in through the door. And don't press any other buttons or you're dead.' All this was said in a very hushed voice. There were two typists at work addressing statements a few feet away and also the deposit box girl at her desk. They heard nothing. As you see, the bank is L-shaped and we are around the corner from the main section, out of sight. No one saw."

"So you opened the door?" said Scott.

"I opened the door and the other man who had been standing back with his hand in his pocket came in. He drew his gun and made the girls and myself get face down on the floor. He said, 'If one of you turns a hair in this direction you'll get it right in the head.' My God, we certainly weren't going to argue the point. We did exactly as we were told."

"Then what happened?"

"We heard some quick movements, heavy breathing as

they wrestled with the sacks, some whispering. Then one of the voices said, 'Okay, Rick. You and Junky load the car and take off. I'll hold a gun on these jerks another five minutes.' After that it was perfectly still. But it wasn't much over a minute before one of the tellers came back on an errand and found us. Of course, the robbers had gone and we turned in the alarm. It didn't seem like two minutes before the first police car arrived. Then the whole area was swarming with them and in no time all the exits from the city were blocked."

"But there never was a single clue?"

"No. The police now have come to believe they calmly loaded the money in a paint truck, drove somewhere and unloaded it with their fake equipment. But not one person can be found who remembers such a truck parked outside or cruising the streets. A woman remembers seeing two painters carrying something down the hall of the building between them. She said it was white and looked like a big folded tarp. Of course the money must have been in it. As you know, there are two entrances to the bank. This one right here in the building corridor. And at the other end, the one to the street. Two people tried to enter here and found a sign which said, *Painters at work, use street entrance*. And that, Mr. Daniels, is how they sealed off this door."

"Neat," said Scott. "They didn't miss a trick."

"Absolutely professional," said Mr. Wilkins. "Timing, costume, escape—all perfect."

"What was the exact amount stolen, Mr. Wilkins?"

"All told, five hundred thousand, seventeen hundred dollars."

"Coffee and cakes for quite a while. About the names you heard—"

"Rick and Junky? Well, of course there are a lot of Ricks with police records. Junky might imply a dope addict. The police are checking—not to successfully, I'm afraid."

"Was there ever any mention of a woman in this case?"

"A woman? No, sir. Not that I know of." Wilkins bore a look of studious perplexity.

"It seems to me," said Scott, thoughtfully, "that the tim-

ing was a little better than professional. Tell me this, does
the name Valerie mean anything to you? Was there ever an
employee by that name in the bank?"

Curiosity shadowed the mild features of Mr. Wilkins. He
kept the question to himself. "I've been here a good many
years," he said, "and I'm pretty sure there was never a girl
we called Valerie. Could you give me the last name?"

"It would be one of the great pleasures of my life," said
Scott. "But I'm afraid I can't."

"If it's important, I could check."

"Would you?"

"Certainly."

Wilkins departed. He returned in a few minutes with a
negative shake of his head. "Sorry. No Valeries in our per-
sonnel records. It isn't a name you hear very often. I do know
of a depositor by that name. A Mrs. Valerie Hobson."

"How old is she?" said Scott excitedly.

Wilkins considered, requesting an answer of the ceiling.
"I'd say about fifty . . . fifty-five at most."

"Damn!" said Scott.

"I beg your pardon?"

"I'm looking for someone younger. In any case, I don't
think she would be a depositor. Wouldn't that be a funny
one. . . .?"

"Mr. Daniels, it would take a bit of time, quite a bit without the last name."

"I wasn't going to ask you. It never occurred to me. But—"

"You'd better have a seat," said Wilkins, smiling. "Right
over there. I'll put a girl on it and call you."

"Thanks," said Scott. "It's all terribly far-fetched. I can't
explain just now. But keep it to yourself, will you?"

Wilkins gave him a wink.

Daniels could not sit still. He went out into the building
corridors and looked around. He made a study of the exits,
the streets they emptied upon, the outside entrance to the
bank. The police must have covered all this ground and a
lot more. With all skill and every possible aid. And yet it was
not ridiculous to suppose that he had a better chance. They

had not a single clue while he had the one big one. Valerie the hub, with spokes of knowledge leading from her.

He had been seated a good half-hour when he saw Wilkins beckoning him. He went to the window.

"We found two more besides Mrs. Hobson," he said. "One in checking and one in saving. If you're looking for a younger woman, you can forget the one in checking. The one in savings was a very small account which was closed out three weeks after it was opened. The lady appears to be twenty-six. There's an address, no phone. The name is Miss Valerie McLean. I've written it down for you." He gave Scott a slip of paper. The address was an apartment building in the southwest section.

"Can't thank you enough, Mr. Wilkins. This is nothing more than a rather silly hunch of mine I have to follow through. Very little hope that anything will come of it."

Wilkins smiled indulgently. "Glad to be of service," he said.

But Daniels did have a very big hope that Valerie McLean, aged twenty-six, would be a most attractive brunette who no longer kept her money in savings but in a great tan suitcase.

TEN

THE GIRL WHO opened the door to apartment seven at the address written on the slip of paper was certainly a brunette. She could also have been twenty-six. But here any similarity ended.

The hair was close cropped, a boyish bob crowning a tiny heart of a face containing huge and glistening dark eyes with that peculiar combination of bold-shy watchfulness associated with children. Small nose and mouth, the latter slightly spread to a smile that looked more habitual than personal.

Costume of the day appeared to be lounging pajamas of pale blue.

"Yes?" she said. The word fell from her mouth without the slightest lip movement.

"I hope I have the right address. I'm looking for Valerie."

"Valerie McLean?"

"That's right."

"Won't you come in a moment?"

The living room was a walk-in closet furnished in period anonymous. A portable ironing board draped with a pink slip was fixed by the window.

She indicated a chair opposite as she fell upon a daybed and drew up her legs. The same diminutive smile hovered about her face.

"You know the old saying?" she opened. "Valerie doesn't live here anymore."

"Oh? Then where does Valerie live?"

She shrugged. "I haven't the faintest idea." Her look said it was a dull subject which should be dispatched quickly for the purpose of probing this new-found relationship.

"I take it," said Scott, "that at one time she was your roommate."

"For less than two weeks. I imagine she found something more to her liking. Valerie is kind of a snob, you know. Or don't you?" She reached for cigarettes and waited for him to make the light, cupping her hands around the flame so that her fingers rested across his wrist. He withdrew discreetly.

"Yes, I suppose Valerie is something of a snob," he said. "But then, I don't know her very well. We met at a party and she gave me this address." He searched frantically for some way to match the identity. "She reminded me so much of a girl I used to know in New York—tall and dark-haired with that haughty way she carries herself. And that voice— the Park Avenue sound, you know, my dear."

"That's Valerie, all right," she said, the words pushing smoke puffs ahead of them. "I don't like to be catty but I used to think that she was a phony. See what I mean?"

"Of course. She's not really my type. But I'm connected

with television and she's tall and slender enough to be perfect for a modeling bit on a show we're doing."

"My name is Shirley D'Amico," she said. "I'm not tall, but terribly, terribly talented. Must you have tall girls, Mr. . . ."

"Daniels. Scott. And yes, I'm afraid I must. But I'll keep you in mind for something else. And now I hate to harp on the same old subject, but I've got to find Valerie right away. Can you help?"

"I wouldn't know where to begin," she said. "You could write what I know about Valerie on your thumb. She answered an ad I put in the paper for a roommate to share expenses. She had nice clothes and Emily Post was her best friend. She had everything—everything but the expenses. And a job. I took her in because she promised to pay her share on the first, out of a trust fund check she said was coming to her. I tried to get her some kind of work, but nothing suited her highness. Then she just bolted into the blue."

"I don't understand."

"Well, I work nights. Cashier at a movie house. I came in on a Thursday around midnight and she was gone. She didn't leave so much as a hair in the sink. Gone."

"A note?"

"Yes. She left a note. *Dear Shirley. Please forgive me, darling. But I had a rare opportunity that will take me out of town for awhile. Hope this will soften the blow.*

"And get this, pinned to the note was a fifty dollar bill. Rare opportunity, indeed!"

"Did she ever get in touch?"

"Never. I never heard from her again. The hell with roommates! I'm a loner from now on."

"Did she have any friends who came here?"

Shirley raised her eyebrows. "My dear man. Of course. But they were always gone when I came home. Nothing but a few tattered cigarette butts, a chewed sandwich and whiskey rings in glasses. She said nothing and I asked no questions. Live it up and let live."

"So you can't tell me one little thing by which I could trace her?"

"Not one. But don't take it so hard. Little old Shirley stands ready to comfort. Valerie would have been expensive. And I'm the homey type."

He looked around. "I'm sure. But come now, Shirley. You must have some clue to her, however vague. Didn't she mention the name of a single friend? I have a special reason."

"She owes you money?"

He looked down.

"That's tough. In which case, I'll try to think." Small fingers touched brow. "Think, think," she said. "A tiny name dawns. But it wouldn't do you a bit of good."

"Please?"

"Well . . . I had a broken watch. Dropped it on the bathroom floor. Valerie said she had a friend who was in the watch repair business and she would get it fixed for nothing. She mentioned someone by the name of Marty. No last name. She took the watch and had it back in a couple of days. That won't help, will it?"

"Hardly," he said dejectedly, already guessing that the name when connected with watchmaking was more than worth the trip.

He stood. Tried to keep impatience from crowding his face. "Well, it wasn't too important, Shirley. Chalk it up to experience. And thanks, anyway."

"Would you like to celebrate the loss with a drink?" It came out urgently casual.

Lonely, he thought. So many like her. "Love to. But I'm on company time and late. Got to run." He went to the door. She came after him on puppet strings, a doll dancing over the floor.

"You're a very pretty man, Scotty. Won't you come back--soon?" She placed hands behind head and arched toward him. "Remember—I'm terribly, terribly talented."

He opened the door. "Yes," he said. "But I'm terribly, terribly married. Goodbye, Shirley."

He slipped out and went down the hall with a fixed image

of Shirley D'Amico's face—the dark, wounded eyes of a fawn, mouth gaping.

Just as though she had been stabbed.

It was ten minutes after one. He hadn't eaten and he wasn't hungry. He stood in the lobby of the Commerce Exchange Building, consulting the directory of offices. He had just called Myra and she had read from the newpaper: ". . . was identified as Martin Bates, who died this morning from injuries sustained in a puzzling two-car accident on Route 27. Mr. Bates, a watchmaker and proprietor of a one-man shop housed in the Commerce Exchange Building, was driving north to. . . ."

But that was enough. Martin. Marty. A friend of Valerie's. In the same accident.

Barnes . . . Bassett . . . Bates, Martin. Rm 406.

He hurried to the elevator.

406 was a small opaque glass door, one of several in a hallway.

MARTIN BATES, WATCH SHOP
Watch and clock repairing, all makes.
Electronic, precision timing.
Fast Service.

And just below this was a hand-printed sign:

CLOSED FOR SUMMER VACATION

Scott Daniels returned to the main floor, all the while thinking, *not coincidence. Not at all. An impossible sequence for coincidence. Marty Bates of the accident. Marty mentioned as a friend of Valerie's. Marty of the watch shop. Where? In the same building as the Second National. Then why not Marty involved in the robbery? Marty and friend. And after the robbery, where would Marty and friend go with the loot for quick escape? Where else? To the Martin Bates Watch Shop.*

He was bursting with excitement. *And yet, Marty is dead. You have a modus and that's all. Where, where is Valerie?*

He went back into the bank and sat down for time to think. It came to him finally. If Valerie opened an account, someone must have talked with her at the time. You fill out the card and the nice man or woman takes your money.

Mr. Scofield was quite a nice man behind one of many desks in a row. He was also a vice president. Why was it that vice presidents in banks never seemed to have their own offices? Anyway, Mr. Scofield had the appropriate dignity and he held the card in his hand.

He smiled pleasantly. "Yes," he said. "I see that this is my signature and so I must have opened the account. It's one of a dozen things that I do in a busy day. But it was some time ago and there are so many. I'm afraid I don't remember the lady. Now, if it had been a large amount. . . ."

"Well, of course," said Scott, "the amount was small. But the lady from almost any view, largely attractive. A tall brunette with a striking figure. Would that help?"

Mr. Scofield allowed himself a polite chuckle. "It should help," he said. "And the point is well taken. But, on the other hand, more often than you might think, we have reasonably attractive young ladies making deposits."

"I think this one is unreasonably attractive, sir."

Mr. Scofield continued to smile tolerantly. "If you know her, Mr. . . . Daniels, is it?"

"That's right."

"Well, if you know her, Mr. Daniels, what's the problem?"

"I've lost her. Temporarily, I hope. And I thought if you could remember her, then you might also remember something she told you which would help me to find her."

Mr. Scofield frowned. "I'm rather confused," he said. "Our head teller, Mr. Wilkins, dug this card out of the files. And he said that you were connected with one of the television stations gathering background for a crime series. Is that so?"

"Yes, sir, that's right."

"And that the first program on the schedule concerns the

recent robbery of this bank. Now, what does that have to do with this Valerie. . ." he looked down at the card, "Valerie McLean?"

"Nothing, really," Scott lied. "It's a personal matter which I thought I would straighten out while I was here."

Mr. Scofield began to tap the card thoughtfully on his thumbnail. "You know, Mr. Daniels," he said, "sometimes a person like yourself nosing around on perfectly legitimate business, comes across a fact or two that might have entirely escaped the police. To say nothing of the uh . . . bank officials. I do think it would be a grave mistake in judgement not to pass on to us immediately the smallest detail, however seemingly unimportant."

"I agree with that, Mr. Scofield. In principle. And if I had something concrete or resolved, I would take it to the police."

"It need not be anything resolved at all, just the merest hint," said Mr. Scofield doggedly and with a countenance that was becoming increasingly stern.

Scott was silent.

"I assure you," said Mr. Scofield after a moment and in a more placating tone, "that anything you tell me will be held in the strictest confidence. In fact, I'll go out on a limb and say that at least for the time being, I would be willing to keep any information entirely to myself."

Scott was tempted. But having come so far alone . . .

"I realize," continued Mr. Scofield with a man-to-man smile, "that there is a substantial reward. It might influence your decision if you knew that as an official of the bank, I am not eligible. On the other hand, I would be glad to work with you and help you evaluate in secrecy for a reasonable period."

Somehow, in a very remote sense, Mr. Scofield reminded Scott of Milt Lundberg. It was an executive attitude, pseudo-friendly double talk laced with a condescension born of years behind fat desks of authority. Scott felt himself being persuaded with an invisible club and his response was a rising irritation.

"Really, Mr. Scofield," he said, "I think you're making much of nothing, if I may say so. I'm just another guy earning a living and my knowledge of crime and criminals is just about what I read in the newspapers. So getting back to my girl friend on the card there—Valerie McLean—have you been able to remember her?"

Mr. Scofield knew that he was being signed off and after a moment in which his big jaw resisted, acceptance came to his face. He looked again at the card.

"Have you checked this address?" he asked.

"Oh, yes. She moved. Not a trace."

"You're not acquainted with any of her friends?"

"I met her just once at a party."

"And the person who invited her, the one who gave the party?"

That was a tough one but it flashed just as he was going to fumble for a cigarette in what might have been an obvious stall.

"Nothing doing," he said. "She wasn't known—except by the man who brought her. And he was a stranger to me."

"Well," said Mr. Scofield dubiously, "it looks pretty hopeless. I can't seem to bring her up out of my mental file. I must talk to twenty or more people a day. Tell you what." He slid paper and pencil across the desk. "Just write your name, address and phone number here for me. Then I'll give it some thought. If and when I can remember, I'll give you a call. However, it's very unlikely that she would have told me anything you could use to trace her. We don't ask for personal details and they're seldom volunteered."

Scott wrote the information and they stood together, shaking hands. "Much obliged, Mr. Scofield."

"Not at all. And, Daniels. Remember my advice. Don't take it too lightly. Anytime you. . . ."

"Sure, sure. I'll do that. The minute I have anything that would interest you. 'Bye, sir."

Scott Daniels moved briskly toward the exit into the building. There was within him a need for tremendous haste. Yet in the corridor he paused. *Hurry!* he thought. *But to where?*

ELEVEN

THE MINUTE Daniel's back disappeared out the door, Clay Scofield wrenched the phone across the desk to call Valerie. He dialed furiously. The ringing went on and on, a drill boring into the side of his head.

He looked at his watch, then hung up. She had driven into town with him for another of her interminable shopping sprees. And he had forgotten that at noon she had an appointment at the hair-dresser's. Probably she wouldn't reach home for another hour.

Daniels. Daniels. . . . It sounded familiar. He grabbed the paper and looked at the scrawled name and address. Scott Daniels. Unless he was mistaken, for he had paid little attention at the time, this was the man who had given Valerie the lift from that joint on 27, then picked up the suitcase.

God, God. Oh, Christ almighty! Even if he wasn't the one, (and he must be, or where did he get the name Valerie?), he was onto some part of it, moving closer. Hadn't he told Valerie to be careful, careful, careful! How could she be so stupid as to drop even her first name? The trouble with women, the whole trouble with any bitch alive was that their intelligence went just so far—and the emotion took over. Except in the case of his wife, Mavis (former wife? Not yet.) who in her whole life probably never had an honest emotion.

And he had slipped, too. He should never have allowed Valerie's card with his own signature on it to remain in the files. The day after the account was closed he could have sneaked it out. But how could he know that it would ever be of the least importance?

Something had to be done about Daniels. And fast! But what? In God's name, what? And on top of it there was Roy

Whalen to deal with—determined, absolutely convinced, relentless.

If he, Clay Scofield, were some goddam criminal, it would be much simpler. He could just disappear with Valerie and the money, right out of the country. But as it was, if even a mop boy, let alone a vice president quit the bank, the whole police force might be right behind him, handcuffs ready. So now the entire, clever, beautifully planned scheme was falling apart. He should have been content with his small share. He should not have been so greedy. But after Mavis got her pound of flesh for the divorce and the loans were paid off, there wasn't enough left to exist on any permanent level that would satisfy him—or the spoiled, hungry tastes of Valerie McLean.

No, the trouble was Mavis, not Valerie. The trouble was first, last and always, Mavis. She had been a wound in his side that he had finally closed with money, money and more money.

In the beginning, eleven years ago when he was an assistant cashier, Mavis had presented quite a different picture. She was the daughter of Harvey Fitzgerald, now dead, but then the president of the bank. Which didn't hurt her standing with him a bit.

She was neither beautifully nor delicately put together. Today he would say she was a goddam gangling horse who would bite the hand that fed it sugar. But then he thought of her as handsome—a tall, bigboned girl with elegant bearing on fine legs, her features classic under an abundance of richly gold-blonde hair.

Mavis Fitzgerald: Quick of mind and speech, a brittle dominant person, knowing exactly where she was going. If there was a bridge party, charity drive or egg roll, she was immediately elected queen, for she was a tireless organizer.

Actually, as Clay discovered too late, she was a fraud. Her whole life was a pose. She covered a great void in areas of sensitivity and depth with much shouting and running about.

She was a superb actress in the clinches, pretending to be

violently sensual with little sobs and gasps, followed by reluctant breakdowns at crucial moments.

But Clay was completely fooled before the marriage and, considering the position of her father, she seemed most impressive. It was not difficult to believe he was in love with her.

Shortly after the ties were made, her acting performance rapidly lost enthusiasm. And he discovered that she was a zombie—cold in bed and out, inherently unable to express a single genuine emotion or affection, though intensely selfish and vain. Because she adored money and despised his lowly position, the only thing she ever did for him was to whip him forward, while urging her father to promote him at every opportunity.

He soon became cashier and finally vice president, one of four in the department of personal loans. Meanwhile they had a child (to Clay, it seemed a wonder that a living thing could come out of that stone of a woman), and Mavis excused her inability to show affection by promptly spoiling the boy.

He would have divorced her if it was not necessary to maintain the relationship in the eyes of her father, thus securing his position at the bank. When her father died, he began an open warfare, hoping that she would make the first move so he could gain his freedom at a bargain price. But nothing could reach a void, and all that developed between them was a growing silence.

Then, through the swinging doors of the bank, walked Valerie McLean. And he no longer just wanted a divorce, he *had* to have it.

He was remembering that singular occasion, when Miss Folmer appeared at his elbow. "You have a customer waiting," she said.

"Who is it, Dorothy? Anyone I know?"

"Just a man who wants to open a checking."

"Give him to Gossard, will you? I'm trying to get through on an important call."

"Yes, sir." She went off.

He picked up some letters that had been placed on his desk for signature and presented a picture of frowning concentration.

It was a matter of luck that Valerie came to his desk. She might have been ushered to any of the loan officers fore and aft of him. But a customer had just departed and for the moment the chair by his desk was vacant.

He watched her approach with immediate excitement. She was neatly and artfully dressed. Slightly haughty, but neither self-conscious nor austere, the expression on her pretty face was one of anticipation, as if she perpetually sought adventure from the smallest event.

She sat down with her slow smile and announced that she would like to open a savings account and was quite flattered to have the personal attention of the vice president. He did not tell her that he was one of eight vice presidents throughout the bank. He merely assured her that opening an account was an important function.

From the grandeur of her dress and manner, he expected that she would offer for deposit a sum anywhere between a thousand and ten thousand. Instead, she opened her purse and slowly counted a hundred dollars in small bills. He took the money blandly and filled out the card. When she had her bankbook and was ready to leave, she gave him the first small glimpse into her character.

"Tell me, Mr. Scofield," she said with apparent naïveté, "is it sometimes possible to obtain a loan for a depositor? I mean, without the usual red tape?"

"Are you speaking of a signature loan? Unsecured?"

"Yes." Her whole face brightened.

He looked at her card and saw no mention of employment. "Do you have income, Miss McLean? Are you employed?"

"Neither," she said. "Not at the moment, that is."

Ordinarily, he would immediately have given her the high-toned, short speech and executive brush. But across the desk her appeal was magnetic, he could look at her for hours without boredom. She was unmarried and possibly available.

"Well," he said, "of course there is always a little red tape.

And generally if there is no income and no collateral, we don't make loans. On the other hand," he added heartily, "there are always exceptions. Why don't you think over how much you would need and then come back and see me. I would be happy to discuss it with you."

"How very kind," she said. "I certainly will, Mr. Scofield."

"Are you looking for work, Miss McLean?"

"Well, yes. As a matter of fact, I am."

"There again," he said. "I may be able to help. Why don't you keep in touch?"

She promised that she would and as she shook hands, the pressure was held that fraction of overtime which told its own story.

She was back in three days asking for five hundred dollars, secured only by her smile. He told her that according to bank regulations this was impossible. But that if he knew her better as a person, something might be worked out. The matter could be discussed that evening over dinner.

She was quite agreeable.

After an evening in which he fell completely in love with her, embraced her passionately and at length in his car, collected promises that the affair would continue, he "loaned" her a hundred dollars out of his own pocket. And there it began.

In the days that followed, he built a somewhat hazy and fragmentary picture of her background and make-up. Evidently she was the product of a completely undisciplined life.

Valerie McLean: She came from Los Angeles where her father made a great deal of money in the black-marketing of overpriced new and used cars during the second war. Went to the best schools, lived on a lavish scale, traveled with a racy crowd. Always in trouble—just missed jail when she began to write large checks on an exhausted bank account.

She couldn't adjust when her father lost his money after the boom with some foolish and desperate speculations.

Moved around from city to city in a world of borderline adventure, scheming more than earning her way.

For men, her body was a promise which seldom paid off. She was particular and some of the worst slobs had the most money. She was not all black—she had charm and cleverness and she was able to give to a very few men, a reckless and inventive passion, affection and even love.

Clay Scofield was one of those few men. And his need for her giving was so insatiable that he was glad to divorce his wife and marry her. She blessed him as a savior until he confessed that to be elected one of eight vice presidents in a bank did not carry with it a contract which said, ". . . and all the money you can use."

Vice presidents in the Second National were as common as tellers. He was a glorified flunky with a title to impress the public. The job, complete with swivel chair, was good for ten thousand five a year. The executive V.P. made fifteen thousand and that was a long jump with seven competitors. It would never be more than a comfortable living.

And there was the problem of Mavis. The worst of all problems. He didn't want to be tied by alimony to that bitch for endless years. He offered to try to raise ten thousand if she would give him a clean bill, no strings. She laughed in his face.

"I can't hold you," she said, "and I don't want you. You can take the house and the car, I'll take Jimmy" (he was nine now), "and forty thousand cash."

"Forty thousand! Where would I get that kind of money?"

"I don't give a damn how you get it. You're a loan officer. Make yourself a loan!"

And that's what he did. Not the impossible way she meant it—the easy way. When Valerie understood his privileges, she suggested it. He could, using fictitious names, approve dummy loans on his signature and collect the cash. If the amounts weren't too large and taken over a reasonable period of time, no one would question.

He got the forty thousand together and sent Mavis packing with her spoiled brat. And while he was at it, he took thousands extra to provide Valerie with an apartment and the style she loved. His total embezzlement was sixty-two thousand.

Stealing the money was nothing to keeping it covered. The notes were short term and were beginning to come due. He had to rob Peter to pay Paul—an endless cycle. It couldn't go on. They would catch him sooner or later.

He was in frantic search of a way out the day he and Valerie, Roy Whalen and Marty Bates became strange drinking partners. The result was the plan. It was an enormous decision and apparently sudden. Yet, it was one for which the evolutions of his subconscious had been preparing for years.

A tortured seed had developed a dangerous fruit. And it was ripe.

Now he lifted the receiver and again dialed Valerie. No answer. He cut the connection and angrily jiggled for the operator. He asked for the head teller.

"Wilkins," he said, in his most executive voice, "what's the story on this man Daniels? Are we giving him carte blanche to take the bank apart? What do you know about him?"

"Nothing much, sir. No more than I told you."

"Why is he looking for some woman named Valerie?"

"He wouldn't say, sir. But I gathered he suspects her of some connection with the robbery."

"Is that so? Well, he's obviously an ass and a nuisance. If he comes back, tell him nothing, just send him to me. Is that clear?"

"Yes, sir."

He hung up.

He clenched the edge of the desk until his knuckles were white. Goddam, goddam! Roy Whalen and now this Daniels. He could handle Whalen because at least Whalen wouldn't talk. But Daniels was another matter.

Daniels would have to be taken care of. And it was going to have to be handled in some final way. That would be messy. He really hated violence. But once he was committed, no matter the direction or consequences, he plunged ahead in the most practical manner and never looked back.

Just as soon as he could reach Valerie there would have to be another decision.

TWELVE

"THEY TELL ME," said Scott to one of the elevator boys whose name was Sam, "that you were about the only one around here who knew Martin Bates very well."

Sam looked like he never had to shave, had the face of a teenager and the build of a jockey. But he must have been forty.

"Nah," he said. "Marty was no friend of mine, if that's what ya mean. He used ta kid me a lot about when I was goin' back ta school 'cause I look so young, he says. Wouldn't take it from nobody else. But he was a pretty good guy. We shot the breeze, that's all. Why?"

"It's a legal matter," said Scott. "We're trying to locate some of his possessions that appear on an inventory list but can't be found. Now, as I understand it, he used to ride your car a lot because it's one out of the only two in his wing of the building."

"Yeah, that's right," said Sam, who that second got a call. "You'll have ta hoist up with me, mister. If ya wanna go on talkin'."

Scott stepped on. The door closed and they ascended. "When Bates got off your car, Sam, did he ever have a suitcase? A big tan one?"

Sam considered as he opened the door, passengers stepped in and they dropped below. He didn't speak until they reached the main floor and the car was empty. "Big tan suitcase? No, sir. I never seen one. Before he went on vacation, though, he took down a whole bunch a packages. Every night a few. Clocks, watches, repair kit, stuff like that.

He tole me he was gonna do some homework while he was visitin' his brother. That's what he says."

"I see," said Scott, who really did see, very well. "Perhaps we could get more information if we could locate some close friend of his in the city. Did you ever notice any one particular person who hung around with him?"

Sam took off his cap and smoothed wisps of hair over a nearly bald pate. He had aged in an instant. "Lemme see . . . well, there was one guy. Roy, I think he called him. They used ta go fishin' together. This guy, Roy, he works for one of them charter boats down to the pier."

"You know the name of the boat, Sam?"

"Nah. They was talkin about it but I didn't pay no attention. Heard 'em say it was one of them fancy four-chair jobs. Kind that costs seventy-five bucks a day. That's not for me, brother. Not if it was seventy-five bucks a month."

"Did Bates have any girl friends?"

"Wouldn't know that. Never seen him with none."

"You can't remember this Roy's last name?"

"Never heard it."

"Okay, Sam. And thanks a lot."

Scott gave him a dollar. Then headed for the pier to look for a nameless charter boat and a man called Roy.

THIRTEEN

Roy Whalen was still waiting, parked with his car just around the corner from Clay's house, nosed forward enough so that he could see Valerie arrive. He had been disappointed when she drove off with Clay that morning. He had expected that she would remain home alone. It was now after one and the time was growing short. He would need a couple of hours with her before Clay came back from the bank.

He knew that in time he could bring enough pressure to bear on Clay, threats of exposure or physical force, to make him talk. But the simple and fast route was by way of Valerie. And much more fun, too. From the very beginning she had been a thorn of irritation—needling an incessant lust which brought daydreams of her unclad image to mind for hours after every meeting with her. The stuff was there behind her eyes—but not for him. And now he would not leave her before that goddam sassy tail had a whipped-dog look and her snooty head hung with humility, acknowledging that he was more man than Clay Scofield—for all his pretty-boy manners and phony dignity.

How he ever got mixed up with a pair like them was little short of miraculous, a goddam quirk of fate, as the man said.

On a day when the sky was a blue gem without a carbon cloud. On a day when the sea was a green quilt along the shore, running to blue in the depths of the Gulf Stream. A day when the hard pull and the swift run of the rainbow dolphin, the jerk and silver flash of the 'cuda, the leap of lancing sail, should all be known to a man in the sport chair of Buck Kingsley's charter cruiser.

Not so, on that day. Clayton Scofield and his babe had given up after a couple of no-fish hours and broken out the bottle. And there had begun the plot for the catching of a half million clams. Just a big joke at first. Until Marty had seen the speculation, the sneaking idea, forming behind Scofield's mask of laughter.

At the time, Roy had been a hook baiter, line setter, gaffer and deck swabber for Kingsley. Peanuts a week. He knew boats and fishing, Buck had lost his helper and needed a new boy. Roy didn't know Kingsley but he walked out on the Municipal Pier and talked into the job.

All his life he had walked around this world talking into jobs—usually hard physical work, anything skilled with the hands. Construction, oil drilling, engine repair, even farm labor. He never stayed long anywhere, because sooner or later someone gave him crap, someone had a big bossy mouth and his pride made him lash back with tongue or fist.

For that reason, and for that reason alone, he was a failure.

He was sharp in the head, quick to learn any stupid job. He could have gone high and fast in any line. But he never could suck around long enough to get on top where he could give the orders.

It was all logical and right that he was his own man. But still, he was a bust and in him there was always the sour, bitter taste of defeat. Something lay wounded inside, patching itself with self-pity, waiting to rise up and fly out at life in one bright moment of revenge. And thus, all of his existence had been undeclared patience for the moment of the plan.

He had known Marty Bates since the one short year they shared in reform school. But while Roy had grown out of his teenage rebellion into more subtle and legal forms of resistance, Marty had shoved on, sometimes gun in hand, to take what was his. Marty was a shrewd operator, cautious and long scheming, and never again had they placed him behind bars.

His father was a watchmaker and taught him the trade. Wherever he went, in the long spells between "jobs" or con games, he used the watch repair angle as a dodge. Marty was one who believed in making a big score, then coasting for long safe months or years.

Marty would often stake Roy when he was broke, and for this reason alone, Roy kept in touch. Roy was very broke indeed when he hit Miami and, as usual, Marty took care of him, brought him into his own apartment. In return, on days when the charter boat put out to sea with an empty chair, Roy would urge Buck to give him the place. Marty was an incurable fisherman and would drop everything when they were biting for free.

And on this clear blue day, with four chairs and only two in use by The Wheel and his classy dame, Marty had been on tap just like a paying customer.

By mid-day a full quart was nearly half shot, the dame was giggling and The Wheel was loosening up around the spokes. Another hour and it was first names, the quart was being passed to all but Buck who didn't drink and remained aloof on the flying bridge because he hated "puking drunks who fished out of a bottle."

A damn good thing Buck was out of earshot, too. Because some words were passed in jest that got serious in two days time and Buck might have put three and two together and come up with a half million.

Roy could see Valerie now, standing there with legs spread against the gentle roll, wearing a tight jersey, pedal pushers and a vague hair-down smile. And saying, "Marty, did you know that you were in the presence of the vice president of the Second National Bank? Get a respectful tone on your mouth and salaam three times."

"That's enough of that, Val," said Scofield. But he drooled when he said it.

"Not the Second National," said Marty. "Well, I'll be goddamned! My shop is in the same crib. Kee-ryst, I keep my small change in there. Clay, old buddy, you got a hundred grand until tomorrow?"

And then much later, Marty again, "Christ, Clay, don't you ever get the urge to clean out the whole goddam vault and thumb your nose at the world—from say, Tangiers?"

Clay with half-smile. "Sure, Marty. But they watch me."

"You ever have anyone stick up the joint?"

"Nope. And they'd never get away with it."

"Why?"

"The little men in blue are geared for it. Close off the whole town in a matter of minutes."

"You think so? Bet I could clean your green and get away with it, easy."

"Big words, my man," said Clay chuckling. "How?"

"I'd wear a wig and a beard and hustle it right upstairs to my little shop. Wait until the wind died and take off."

"Clever," said Clay casually. "You're in the wrong racket." But before he looked down into his glass, a small flicker of interest crossed his face. So Marty pursued.

"Of course," he said, "I'm just pulling your leg. And a guy would never get away with it. Every teller with a gun, guards all over the place."

"I can see you're not up on banks in this town," said Clay, burping behind his hand. "Not ours, anyway." He leaned forward. "I'll tell you something in strictest confidence. Our tellers are not paid to risk their lives and not one of them has a gun. Every dime in that bank is insured. So we have a policy, comes right down from the top. We say to every new teller, "If there's a hold-up, don't ever try to be a hero. Do exactly as you're told. Give the criminals every possible assistance on their way. Get them out of the bank before an employee or customer is killed. If there is any shooting, it will be done by the police, outside of our doors."

"You're kidding!" said Marty in amazement. "Crazy."

"Not at all. Why should we risk our lives for money that's insured?"

"What about the guard?"

"Same thing. He carries a gun, of course. But he's window dressing. Just a threat. No shooting. Unless, of course, he does it outside."

Marty took another drink and began to nod his head. "Well, sure. I can see how that makes sense. You got trigger-happy characters snappin' off shots in a tight area like a bank, some innocent pigeons are gonna fall. The cash is insured, why chance it? Give the little men a helping hand. Play Santa and then let the cops pick them off on the streets."

"Exactly," said Clay.

"Jesus," said Marty with an alcoholic grin. "It sure does strike me funny, though. Give the little men a helping hand with that cash. And make it snappy!" He began to chuckle. "Tell you, Clay buddy. You tip me when there's a real big pile in the till, and me and my friend Roy here, will knock it over and split with you."

"That's not funny," snapped Clay. "I don't like that kind of talk. A joke's a joke, but. . . ."

"And he's not joking, are you, Marty?" said Valerie, falling into a chair with a silly smile.

"Oh, well now, for God's sake, of course I'm joking. What the hell you think I am?"

"All right then, drop it," said Clay.

"I'll tell you this, though," said Marty, watching Clay with a fixed and careful look. "You get as holy as you want about it. But there ain't many guys in this goddam world who wouldn't loot your bank or any other bank—providing they were pretty damn sure of getting away with it. And especially providing it was worth their while, a big enough haul to retire for life. And I'm no phony. I'll admit I'm one of those guys."

"Fine," said Clay. "I get the point. So now let's drop it. What we need is another drink all the way round. Val, pass the bottle."

All this time Roy had been watching and listening in silence. He had not entered much in the conversation and had only one drink because he was a hired hand and every now and then Buck would peer below from the bridge. He might lose his small job and he was sick of losing jobs. But he had every reason to know that Marty was perfectly serious. Nor had he missed the interest which Clay had tried to hide with that self-righteous denial. That was the key. If the farthest thing from a man's mind is to rob a bank, why does he have to haul in sail like a wounded preacher?

When they compared notes later, Marty said he got exactly the same impression. Marty could see an open road if it was handled right. So when they debarked, half-loaded and everyone chummy again, Marty said why didn't he and Clay have lunch together come Monday, since they were in the same building. Clay said it was a great idea and they set up the date. Which was another tip off, because Clay and Marty had about as much in common as Park Avenue and The Bowery. And Clay knew it. Both men had read each other like billboards at ten paces.

According to Marty, that lunch with Clay was a regular shell game with words. Scofield was running scared and wouldn't take the bait until about the third martini. That was when Marty slowly pulled the shade up on the window of his life and let Scofield see what he had guessed all along, that Marty was no stranger to the ways of the professional

stick-up artist. Then they both began to lay their cards on
the table. And after a couple more meetings, the whole
deal was hatched.

Meanwhile, Marty was also working on Roy to go in with
him. Usually Marty worked alone. He claimed it was the
best safety insurance he ever had. But this time he had to
have help. Roy refused point-blank. At first. Until Marty
showed him that it was not the beginning of a crime partner-
ship—but a one-time plot that would culminate in a life
of perpetual ease. Scofield had promised he could finger
a half-million payroll delivery for them with no risk of a
gun fight within the bank.

Marty and Roy were to split three hundred seventy-five
grand. Scofield was to get a hundred. And Valerie, for her
small part, was to have the remaining twenty-five thousand.
The overage of seventeen hundred would be split among
them. Scofield was damn unhappy about his cut. But Marty
insisted that the biggest shares should go to those who took
the greatest risk. All Scofield had to do was supply information, watch from his desk for the delivery, then pick up
the phone and dial Marty and Roy, waiting upstairs in the
watch shop.

When Roy saw that it was an astonishingly workable plan
with a minimum risk, he began to break down. In the end,
he decided that he never had and never would amount to
anything. That he would always be at the mercy of some
joe like Buck Kingsley for a handout job. Might as well
give the dice of his life that one big roll—win or lose.

The disguise had come about when Marty had seen some
painters working in the travel bureau office on the main
floor. They would rope off a section and spread a tarp to
protect the area. It seemed perfect. Banks had to be painted,
too. Valerie went all the way to Palm Beach to buy the
coveralls, caps, brushes and tarp. These were antiqued with
dirt and paint spatterings.

The mask arrangement was beautiful for its simplicity.
Strips of black cloth with eye-hole cuttings were sewn inside
the caps. Lift the cap from the head, give it a shake and the

mask, secured at one end, would fall to cover your face.
When not in use the mask became an invisible lining for
the cap. As an added disguise, Marty alone wore horn-
rimmed glasses and a mustache. This was on the outside
chance that even in that incongruous garb, he might be rec-
ognized by a building employee during the short walk down
the hallway from staircase to bank and return. Both men
kept their heads lowered and their attention on the tarp
during this passage. The disguises were smuggled into Marty's
shop at an earlier date.

The execution of the plan was a matter of timing and
coordination. If there was an unforeseen development, they
could still retreat in disguise, right up to the moment they
approached the bank. But there was no hitch.

On that Thursday morning, both men waited behind the
locked door of Marty's shop, from which hung a sign—
CLOSED. The costumes were wrapped for carrying, the
tarp folded inside a huge shopping bag. When the phone
rang and Scofield said, "We have your note, ready to sign,
Mr. Garson," they knew that the guards had just come into
the bank with the money. From his position near the bend
of the L, Scofield could just see a corner of the door—
enough.

The guards would remain a minute or two while the
sealed sacks were checked and signed for by the head
teller, Wilkins. During that time, Roy and Marty in street
clothes, went with their packages to the seldom used stairway. They opened the door from the hall and before it
swung shut, pressed the push-button lock so that no one
could enter from that floor. Now they tore at packages,
pulled the costumes over street clothes, placed bag and
wrappings in the tarp and refolded it, carried tarp, paint
brushes and PAINTERS AT WORK sign in hands.

Quickly they went below, out the main-floor exit, heads
bent during the short walk to the bank entrance. Nearby,
Valerie waited, glancing at her watch as though expecting
to meet someone. This was the signal that the guards had

left the bank and that as far as she could see, the path was clear.

Next they casually placed the sign on the door, took the tarp and backed inside. At the approach of policeman or guard, anyone who looked like trouble, Valerie was to tap on the glass of the door with a coin.

The instant the door closed, as they faced the corridor, they flipped the masks into position. Now they turned around, each with gun in hand. Marty went right to the head teller's window with the tarp, while Roy remained just out of sight but in position to cover anyone entering from the main section of the bank where the elderly guard made a lazy patrol.

Marty forced the teller to admit him behind the rail and in seconds had him and the few employees near him, face down on the floor. Then he unfolded the tarp, gathered the sacks and wrapped them inside. He heaved the canvas covered bundle over to Marty saying clearly, "Okay, Rick. You and Junky load the car and take off. I'll hold a gun on these jerks another five minutes." This gimmick had a double purpose—to keep the employees down while they got away and to lead the cops to believe two of the men, called Rick and Junky, made their escape by car.

But Marty sneaked out quietly. At the door, both men flipped the masks, stowed guns in pockets. Again as painters, this time carrying heavy equipment in a tarp between them, they made their way to the stairway entrance. When no one was watching, they slipped inside and rushed the loot to the fourth floor. Behind the same locked door, they removed costumes, tossed everything under canvas.

Meanwhile, Valerie had taken the elevator to the fourth and was playing lookout in the hall. She had already unlocked the door to the watch shop. Now her coin tap on the door told them they could risk the fifty feet or so distance from stairway to shop. A push of the cross-bar and the door unlocked, they stepped out with their burden and rushed it into the shop. Had they been seen, at least they were in street clothes.

Valerie went around to the other side of the building and took an elevator below. Roy remained with Marty, helping him wrap the money in cardboard boxes which were in turn placed in a chest. Next, they cut the canvas tarp, the sacks, the costumes into small strips. These in turn were boxed and placed in the chest. The chest was heavily locked.

Roy, who had several days before quit his job with Buck Kingsley, now also departed, losing himself in the crowds on the street.

And Marty opened his shop for business.

The rest was no problem. Roy came back the next day and took a couple of the packages. Marty brought the rest home with him in two nights. The scraps of costume were burned, the split made at Marty's. And all the while the progress of the police, or lack of it, was reported to them by Clay Scofield.

It was decided that Roy should move out ahead and check the roads. Marty would follow with the three hundred seventy-five grand. Remaining in the shop until the last minute, he might gather news of any change in police method that would affect their escape.

Not a word of the plan for travel and banking the money had been told to Clay or Valerie.

Even as Roy sat in the car and wondered how it was possible that those two could have figured a way to cross a pro like Marty, a taxi pulled to the curb and Valerie alighted. Her heels went clipping down the walk. She looked crisp and expensive. Her breasts beneath the thin material of her dress bounced with her stride.

Thoughts of the money receded and hung on the back rim of Roy's consciousness. The lust was crowding in, needling him again. And never before had there been such an opportunity.

He watched her fumble with keys, unlock the door. His last image was of that high saucy rump disappearing inside.

FOURTEEN

"WE GOT A couple of Roys around here," said the man in the booth on the Municipal Pier. "Least we did. One of 'em quit. Which one you want? Roy Pardo?"

"He work on one of these charter boats?" asked Daniels.

"Nope. Speedboat rides. You must mean Roy Whalen. He was mate on Buck Kingsley's rig. Gone now."

"Where?"

"Don't know. Heard he got a job back north. Construction. Buck would tell you."

"Where'll I find him?"

"You won't. Not today. Hauled a charter over to Bimini. Catch him here in the morning sometime, I expect. Whyn't you save yourself a trip. Give 'im a call. Number's on this card, take it along."

"Thanks," said Daniels.

"Don't mention. Buck Kingsley, skipper of the *Blue Sail*."

"Thanks again."

"Don't mention."

Scott Daniels, moving off the pier, pulled a handkerchief from his pocket and wiped his brow. The excitement seeped out of him. This looked like a dead end. If Roy Whalen was connected, so what? Back north. East . . . west . . . nowhere. A nowhere lead. Time was escaping.

He felt the dull edge of depression. And just a few steps away there was the cool bar offering the sweet bitterness and spirit thrust of the dry martini. Brilliant thoughts and high purpose on the third one.

Indecisively he altered course. Then swung back again towards his car. Not that road, he thought. The next step down will be sixty per at Recordmill Junction, sweep up when she kicks off the air. Thanks a lot, Dick Hurley, for the suggestion. And Milt Lundberg for the helping hand. But no thanks.

He climbed in the car and cranked up for home.

FIFTEEN

JUST BEFORE SHE opened the door, Valerie had the distinct impression that the phone was ringing. She made haste, but once inside there wasn't so much as an overtone of bell sound. She must have been mistaken. Only Clay would call and then not unless there was an emergency.

She went into the bedroom, the one she shared with Clay. For a moment she studied herself in the dresser mirror. They had done very nicely with her hair. Of course, it was set too tightly. But she would comb it out and brush it thoroughly, restore that fluff which gave her such a casual look of perfection. And oh, the clothes she had bought at Burdine's! Hundreds of dollars worth. A few days for minor alterations and Clay would be in for a surprise.

Lord, it was hot! She unzipped her dress and pulled out of it. She felt sticky. A luke-warm bath with some of those sweet-smelling crystals in the tub and she would be relaxed and fresh again. You went from air-conditioning out into that hot sun and the contrast was just too much.

In the bathroom, while the tub was filling, she removed bra, panties and stockings. Naked, she dumped a few of the crystals in the water and climbed in, readjusting the mixture for more cold.

In a minute she closed the tap and lay back, sinking under. She felt the muscular tension leave her, but the hollow drawn feeling in her stomach remained. Fear. Ugly, ugly. Not until they left this town would it ever vanish. Not until the bank and the police and Roy were just vague little memories of an unpleasant dream.

Roy. He was the one to fear. Neither the bank nor the police had the slightest chance of linking Clay with the robbery—even if they knew who committed it. There was no visible connection. But Roy, by some crude instinct, had

90

come close to the answer of what happened to the money. And then all he had to do was accuse and read the possibilities on Clay's face. Anyway—he knew. Not how. But he knew. And he was going to get that money, whatever it cost him. Or them.

She almost wished Roy was dead and there was Marty to reckon with. She had maneuvered Marty once and might have been able to do it again. He sounded and acted tough. But he had a soft spot for the right woman. Didn't she know?

In Roy she had read pure animal lechery. But in Marty the lechery had been mingled with respect and a little core of something you might call love if you understood his capacity. All she had to do was play up to him on Clay's advice. Nothing open. Just a hint in the eye, a brush against him, an innuendo of conversation. Next thing you know, Roy had gone and Marty was on the phone. He had something to say to her. Would she come over?

And then he was pleading with her to skip with him, showing her the lure of that tan suitcase full of money, explaining the plan. And she was asking a few very indirect questions and getting direct answers, while stalling. She couldn't go with him now because there were loose ends. She had given Clay her share of the money and had to get it back. Also, she was too kind-hearted. She wanted to let him down easy—not just disappear. She would fly to the coast and meet Marty as soon as she got his letter. And, "No, dear, not now. Save that for later when the strain is off us." But she permitted him a few quick caresses to allay his suspicion. And "What time are you leaving, Marty—in case I should change my mind?"

Then she took back to Clay the entire scheme, route and all.

Suddenly she sat up in the tub and listened. It was the second time she thought she heard knocking. For some silly reason you hardly ever found a home down here with a doorbell. People had to break their hands to get your attention.

She heard the sound again. Oh well, probably some salesman. . . . She sank back and began to soap herself.

Clay had been terribly angry about the split in the first place. He should get a full fifty percent because without his information there would be no robbery, no knowledge of the half million and exact moment of its arrival. But he was over a barrel. He had to pay back the sixty-two thousand in fake loans. That left him only thirty-eight, not counting her twenty-five thousand. Which was strictly hers. Strictly. And Clay wanted to use Valerie to find out what Marty and Roy were doing with all that money. His mind was already at work.

Then when he got a picture of Marty traveling alone with the money he came up with a perfectly marvelous, almost foolproof idea to take it away from him. Without his knowing how it was done—if he lived. And Roy just as much in the dark. What Clay did was to steal a car that couldn't be identified by Marty, a car that wouldn't even be missed. The car was in the garage of the big house and the people were gone. Clay told the locksmith he had lost his keys and the man made two complete sets. Then together they drove the Cadillac to Marty's. Waiting in the darkness, they watched him leave.

They took another route for awhile, a short cut. And got ahead of him. It was easy to figure his approximate traveling time since he wouldn't dare run a mile over the speed limit. Out in the open country of the Everglades, they waited on a side road. As they waited there was a brief torrential downpour which must have delayed Marty, for he was later than expected. But eventually the familiar cream and red Olds flashed by. They gave it time, then pulled back on the highway and caught up. Marty was doing exactly sixty. They passed, Valerie on the floor, Clay with a hat pulled down on his head. Just a precaution. It was too dark to identify anyone.

They sped on ahead for a little over a half hour at eighty, figuring Marty to be just a few minutes behind. They came to the gas station joint and Clay let Valerie walk from the intersection over to it as, out of sight, he swung around. She was to wait twenty minutes, though it shouldn't take over ten since both cars would be speeding towards each other. Then she was to figure on trouble and take the bus or any other transportation she could get back to the house.

Originally she was to be in the car for the wrecking of Marty so that she could drive down the road and circle back while Clay got the money, assisting him in any way possible. But waiting for Marty in the rain, Clay changed his mind. Though he was an excellent driver and had the element of surprise in his favor, bad luck might befall him— just as it did. Valerie could have been hurt.

And now when all was done and the danger should have passed, it might be just beginning again.

Valerie got out of the tub and slowly dried herself. She had just covered her nakedness with a negligee, when over the gurgle of the drain, she heard muted splintering of glass. It sounded like it came from the rear of the house. At the same time, the phone began to ring. Frantic, she didn't know which way to run. But she had to determine the cause of that sound. She went to the back door just as Roy Whalen came smirking towards her from the kitchen. Distantly, the phone rang on and on.

"Don't you ever answer a knock?" said Roy, following as she backed off, not for a moment missing the way her body must be revealed through the flimsy dressing gown.

"Are you crazy!" she cried. "Did you have to break a window?"

"Would you have opened the door, sweetheart?"

She could only stare at him, seeing in the glacial brightness of his eyes nothing but sensual cruelty. The phone, with a final angry trill, stopped ringing.

"What do you want, Roy?"

"What do you think?"

"You're wasting your time. You can talk with Clay. He'll be here any minute now," she lied. "Until then, please get out."

"Make me. His hand dropped on her shoulder, his fingers

kneading her flesh. Fear clutched and paralyzed her. Fingers sought the neck of the gown and slid under.

"Don't, Roy. Please!"

"I can't hear you." He was thoughtful. "Don't you think," he mused, "that I'm in a unique position? How many guys ever have it so good? Because what could you do? Call the police?" He snickered. "No, don't run. You wouldn't get three steps." With a quick down-slice of his finger he caught the sash and applied pressure until it came undone. The gown opened.

"That's the trouble, Valerie. On this side of the law where can you turn? Except to one of us. Clay? Don't kid me. I give him a couple of hours yet. Marty's dead. So that leaves just you and me, baby. All by ourselves."

"You wouldn't enjoy it, Roy. I'd fight you every step."

Strangely, if she wasn't so frightened, she might have enjoyed it herself. For every now and then she became curious about these physical types within whom whirled a dynamo of force, silent and unseen, but charging the air with a feeling of stored energy.

"That's where you're wrong," said Roy. "I'd get a boot out of taking it from you. On the other hand, be smart. Cooperation would be safer. Much safer. I could get carried away."

She saw instantly that he was right. A hideous idea was defining itself in her mind.

"Is this what you came for, Roy?"

"It was an afterthought," he said. "But it kept growing on me." He smiled, a humorless twist of the lips. "So it must have been there all the time." He ran his hand along her thigh. "I came for two things. One of them was the money. But I'll get both of them, Valerie. If I have to kill you to do it."

He meant it. There was no room for doubt in the set of his jaw. Of course, the money would be more difficult, resting as it was in a half-dozen safety deposit boxes around Palm Beach. But looking in the mirror of Roy's eyes, she saw herself producing the keys, and then the ride in his car to some motel. And in the morning, Roy waiting behind her as she signed, opened boxes, delivered. All the signatures hers, since Clay had not dared show himself. And all the policemen in their cars and on the streets, beyond calling.

"I should really attend to business first," Roy continued. "Business before pleasure. But somehow, I can't seem to concentrate. Isn't that a funny one?"

"Then hurry," said Valerie. "You're driving me insane!" She choked a sob.

"Insane with passion," said Roy. "Just can't wait for me, baby. Is that it?"

He wrenched the gown off her shoulders. It slithered to the floor. "Goddam. Goddam, now." He whistled. "What I've been missing all these years. Man, oh man!"

She turned her back on him and walked slowly towards the bedroom, knowing he'd follow.

"Jesus," said Roy as he closed the door. "Right in your own little nest—you and lover boy. Ain't that sacrilegious!"

She pulled down the cover and got between the sheets. Then she waited, turning her head as he began to undress.

It was in those moments when he was most oblivious that her hand sneaked over to the night table and slowly eased back the drawer. The steel bulk of the .45 seemed immense and so much heavier than when Clay showed her its operation, saying, "Now if that bastard comes looking for trouble while I'm gone, don't let him get near you. He's dangerous and you wouldn't have a chance with him, Val. I mean that. Now this is fully loaded, safety off. You pull this hammer back and then all you do is squeeze the trigger . . ."

She understood this. But only in a vague sense, the awful power and dreadful finality in the use of such a weapon.

As she lifted the pistol in her hand, thumbing back the hammer, it occurred to her that she might merely threaten him. But she saw with certainty that one way or another, the gun would change hands. She turned towards him and brought the barrel of the gun an inch above the top center of his head.

Then she squeezed the trigger.

She had a confused, multi-impression of pistol jerking

upward in hand, an explosion of terrifying depth and re-verberation, the smell of cordite, and finally the small in-congruous sigh, as Roy Whalen exhaled his last breath.

Her next impression was of a sight so shocking that it would be engraved upon her subconscious, ready to leap into unwelcome view the rest of her days. For the bullet had gone through the top of his head and thundered on to blast away his lower jaw.

With a tortured moan, she turned her head and the weight of the gun, no longer sustained, carried her hand to rest across his shoulder. The feel of his flesh was revolting and she snapped her hand away, allowing the weapon to sink to the bed.

With her back to him, feet on the floor, she sat doubled over, weeping. The phone on the table came into misty vision and she reached for it, lifting the receiver. Her hand trembled so badly that she mis-dialed and had to try again. Finally she got the bank and then Clay.

"Come home," she sobbed. "Come home . . . I don't care how it will look!" she screamed hysterically. "You've got to, you've got to!" Then she hung up.

And sat staring at the receiver with its finger-smear of blood.

SIXTEEN

SCOTT AND MYRA came out of the movie house three blocks from their apartment. Scott bought a paper, glanced at the headlines and tucked it under his arm. They began to walk for home, lights of the thoroughfare fading as they turned the corner. In the smother of heat they ambled west along a shabby street of gloomy buildings.

"I've seen better flickers on TV," said Myra.

"On the late, late, late show," said Scott. "They shouldn't can stuff like that. They should freeze it. Before it gets too ripe for the public digestion. What a waste of time. I should be pole-vaulting off in all directions and I watch a stinking movie that we wouldn't run on a test at three AM."

"Cool in there, though," said Myra.

"Sure. Why do you think we went? We bought a buck's worth of air, slightly conditioned."

"Besides," declared Myra, "you can't do a thing until tomorrow."

"That's right," Scott muttered. He was thoughtful.

They lapsed into silence.

A block from the apartment, heads down, both lost in thought, they began to cross the street.

There was a sudden flare of light, scream of tires, the harsh whine of motor acceleration. They paused in midstreet, turned. Headlights. A shower of brilliance rocketing towards them with a vicious snarl of sound.

"Back!" he shouted, grabbed her wrist and ran with her. They were on the walk—he all but flung her there. The car seemed out of control. It veered toward them, leaping the curb. He gave Myra a gigantic shove, sent her sprawling. Momentum carried him on. The front fender grazed his hip, spun him around. He lost balance and fell as the rear wheels flew past, up over the curb and down again, the car careening back to the street and gunning away.

"Baby!" he said, leaning over her, "you all right?"

"All right," she said weakly. "Just a skinned kneecap."

He helped her up. "Goddam fool!" he said. "Drunk. Some teenage, no-license bastard whose old man should have creamed him long ago. Could have killed you!"

"What about you?"

"Me too, brother. Me, too. Couldn't see the tags. Looked like a Plymouth sedan, though. Three, four years old."

They began to walk again, Myra hobbling for a moment. This time they peered in all directions before crossing.

"Let me see that knee," he said in the kitchen as she made coffee. She smiled and turned one leg towards him, lifting her skirt. "Not just a run," she said. "Home run. Another pair of stockings shot."

"Never mind the stockings," he muttered. "They don't sell knees at the corner store." He leaned down and inspected. "Not bad. Little scab, maybe. Heal right up."

He stood. They looked at each other. He grabbed her and held tight. "My God, my God," he moaned. "What would I do without you? That was close, close. So close."

She kissed him, wrinkled her face, making light of it. "Next time I'll wear knee guards. You know, those ice hockey things. Can't you picture it?" She saw that his face was grim, said, "I love you, you big life-saving oaf."

He grinned, but the grin faded quickly and his face took on a frowning pensiveness as he sank onto a battered kitchen chair. "You know," he said, "I have a weird feeling. In the calm of this little kitchen, the whole thing doesn't seem so accidental."

"Your overworked imagination is showing, dear."

"No. No, it isn't. Showing, but not overworked," he said solemnly. "In the first place, that car wasn't racing down the street. It just appeared. From nowhere. No lights approaching from a distance. You don't see them at all. And then— flash! And you do. Why? Because nine chances out of ten the car was either parked, or moving blacked out."

"I still think you're. . . ."

"And when you hear that kind of engine rev and gear whine, you can bet the guy is in low or second gear for fast takeoff. And what does that spell in big red letters?"

"Yes, but. . . ."

"And if that doesn't sink it, try this. If the guy was drunk or just plain speed-happy, when we ran back likely he would ram ahead on the same course. Oh, no. He follows us like radar, tracking right over the curb. I say that guy was waiting and ready for a kill."

She turned from the stove and stared at him steadily. "Now you've got *me* believing it. I think you're right. But why would anyone want to kill us?"

"Not us—me. Though if you happened to be in the way . . . ."

"You mean someone guessed that you know too much about the robbery?"

"It's a deadly way to get the message," he said. "But they've told me that I'm on the right track. And yet all I've done is ask a few questions of some perfectly respectable people. Unless Valerie herself . . . I don't know. But I'm going to have to talk with Bill Hoag pretty damn soon."

"The detective?"

"Uh-huh. I'm worried, hon. I never thought you'd get involved in this thing."

"I just happened to be there."

"And so was the mayor of Chicago. He just happened to be there when the guy tried to pick off Roosevelt and shot him instead."

"It wouldn't happen again."

"Maybe. But just the same. . . ."

"Come on, dear. Drink your coffee and let's go to bed. There's nothing we can do tonight."

"Tomorrow I'll get hold of this Kingsley guy," he mused. "He seems about the last hope. And then I'll make a deal with Hoag. All right, let's go to bed."

Sleep was only a thin veil between dream and reality. The urgent bell-clatter of the phone brought him awake instantly. He snapped the bed lamp and as he yanked the receiver, glanced at the clock. It was twenty after eleven. He hadn't been asleep a half hour.

"Hello."

"Mr. Daniels?"

"Yes."

"This is Mr. Scofield."

"Who?"

"Clayton Scofield of the Second National Bank." The voice was crackling with strain.

"Well, my God, what is it?" Myra turned in the bed but didn't awaken.

"Hate to call you at this hour, Daniels. But it was too hot to sleep and lying here, I suddenly remembered."

"Remembered what, Mr. Scofield?"

"That McLean woman. Valerie McLean."

"No!"

"Yes. Yes, it all came back to me."

"Tell me, then."

"I'd rather not discuss it on the phone, Daniels."

"Well, I can't see any harm. This is a private line and—"

"Believe me, Daniels, I have my own very good reasons."
His voice was strident, hammering the words.

"Very well. In the morning, I could. . . ."

"It won't hold for morning, Daniels. Why don't you hop
over here now and we can discuss it privately?"

"Well, I don't know," he said, looking at Myra. She was
again sleeping peacefully. He could not possibly leave her
under the circumstances. "Ordinarily, I'd leap at the chance,
Mr. Scofield. But we've had a bad scare here tonight. I
couldn't leave my wife."

"Bring her along, then. If you must."

"Well. . . ." Myra with him in the car, traveling the
dark streets to wherever Scofield lived. En route, anything
could happen. "No, sir, I'm afraid it just can't be done tonight. But I'll be at your desk the minute the bank opens."

"I can't talk to you at the bank!" Scofield said angrily.

"Meet you for lunch, then."

There was an interminable silence.

"Are you still there?"

"Yes, yes. I'm thinking. Don't you want that reward,
Daniels?"

"Of course, but. . . ."

"You see, I have a document here I want to show you. It
seems absolutely incriminating. With a little information from
you, the whole rotten business could be broken. I would
strongly advise you to put aside any personal problems for
the good of the community and drive right on over to my
house tonight."

"Sorry. I have more than myself to consider."

Another silence.

"You're making a serious mistake. I don't like this delay."
He said nothing.

"Can you meet me here, let's say five o'clock tomorrow afternoon? Sharp."

"Tomorrow at five?" Myra could go home with one of the girls at her office. "Yes. I could certainly do that. Give me your address and I'll be there right on the dot."

"It's 3728 Bayview Drive. Can you remember that?"

"Sure. 3728 Bayview. I'll be there."

"It's one of the islands. Take the MacArthur Causeway."

"Right."

"And come alone, Daniels. Meanwhile, I pledge you to absolute secrecy. Do I have your word?"

God! What a pompous ass. "Sure. My word. At five, then. Goodnight."

He hung up.

He lighted a cigarette and found Myra peering at him through slitted eyes. "What is it?" she said sleepily. "Were you talking on the phone?"

"In the morning," he said. "Go back to sleep, hon."

Slowly the lids fell and in a moment she was breathing in the steady rhythm of slumber.

He doused the light and went over to the window. He looked up and down the dark street. It was empty of pedestrians or traffic. For a long time he stood there smoking.

Then he went back to bed.

SEVENTEEN

"YEAH, THIS IS Kingsley. What can I do for you?" On the phone the voice of the *Blue Sail's* owner had a sound that was at once weary and amiable. Myra had long since gone to work and Scott was alone in the apartment.

"My name is Daniels," he said. "Friend of mine asked me to look up Roy Whalen. Know where I can find him?"

"Can't help you there, fella. He hasn't been with me for quite awhile now. Told me he had a big offer back north.

Jersey, I think he said. Supervisor with some construction outfit. Don't ask me the name. He left me in a spot. Didn't give me but a few days notice. Okay by me—if he got a good break."

"Uh-huh. Well, did he have any friends I might contact for his address? I'd like to drop him a line."

"Just one that I ever met. A Marty Bates. Dead now. Poor bastard got it in a smash-up."

"I read about it in the paper," said Scott. "Damn shame. I understand he used to go out with Roy on your boat."

"Yup. Free ride. Took him as a favor to Roy. Listen, I don't want to shut you off but I just pulled in from Bimini and I'm kind of busy getting my rig cleaned up so I can hit the sack."

"Won't keep you but a minute or two more. When was the last time Roy and this Marty shipped out with you?"

"Well, let's see . . . got it. June. Towards the end of the month. Won't forget that trip."

"How come?"

"Oh, some local big-shot and his cookie got real chummy with Marty and Roy. Broke out a bottle, passed it around. Everyone got pretty sloppy. Except me and Whalen. I don't go for this bottle fishing."

"Crazy," said Scott. "A seventy-five-buck corkage charge when they could drink it at home for nothing."

"Sure. Well, this guy was loaded. Gave me a hundred. Peeled it off a fat roll. Listen, pal, I better sign off."

"Who was this guy with the roll?" Scott was suddenly interested.

"He worked for some bank. Maybe owned it, for all I know."

"You don't remember his name, do you?" Scott was now fascinated.

"They're all John Doe to me. Spelled d-o-u-g-h. Why? Thought you were looking for Roy."

"Roy and anyone who ever talked to him."

"He must owe you money."

"In a way. I wish to hell you could remember that guy's name."

"You call back tomorrow and I could locate it for you. I keep a little reservation book. Name and phone number. In case I have to cancel in bad weather."

"You couldn't get that name for me now, could you?"

"Is it really important? Because listen, you're talkin' to one beat sailor. Book's in the cabin and I'm down at the other end of the pier."

"It's important. You get that name and I'll send everyone I know to your boat for charter."

"Deal. Just hold on."

He was gone for what seemed like an eternity. Then, "Hello, Daniels? Here you are. No first name. Just the initial C—C. Scofield."

"Wow!"

"Wow—how? You want the phone number?"

"Sure do." Scott plucked a pen from his shirt.

"Beach 4-7-1-7-0. Got it?"

"Got it. And many thanks."

"Don't forget the *Blue Sail*."

"I'll ride 'er to hell and back myself. Wait, now. Something else. Did you say Scofield had a girl with him?"

"Sweetest sack of cookies you ever saw."

"But no name?"

"Jane D-o-u-g-h."

"What'd she look like?"

"Tall job. Slender chassis, full-house upstairs. Black hair. Kind of hoity-toity—except when she's loaded."

"How old?"

"Oh, she'll be looking back on twenty-five. Not far back, though."

"Name wasn't Valerie, was it?"

"Can't say."

"Much obliged. You've got a bunch of free advertising."

"Deal. See ya, pal."

"So long."

Scott sat looking at the phone for a long time. Then he dialed the station. "That you, Millie?"

"Sure is. Sounds like Scott Daniels. Thought you were on vacation."

"Of a kind. Strange kind. Millie, are you busy?"

"So-so."

"Will you do me a favor?"

"Try, Scott."

"I want you to fake a call for me."

"Why, Scott!"

"Play it straight, it's important. Can you set up a three-way on the switchboard so I can listen?"

"Easy."

"All right. Call Beach 4-7-1-7-0 and. . . ."

"Beach 4-7-1-7-0?"

"Yes. Now I just want to see who's there, if anyone. When the party comes on, pretend you made a goof, any excuse to keep the person talking a few seconds. I'll be listening, but not breathing. Okay?"

"Okay. Such intrigue! But I won't tell your wife."

She dialed and he heard it ring, three, four times. Then a female voice. "Hello."

"Long distance operator," said Millie blandly. "I have a call for Mr. George Johnston."

"Well, I'm sorry, but you must have the wrong number."

"Isn't this Beach 2-7-1-7-0?"

"No. This is Beach 4."

Click. And she was gone. But the voice was young and throaty with overtones of pseudo-culture. He was almost certain it was Valerie.

"Well done, Millie. You're on me for a double-deck hamburger and coffee."

"I'll remind you. Got a call now. 'Bye, Scott."

He got up and and began to pace the room. If ever he needed a drink . . . He went out to the kitchen and opened a bottle of beer. He gulped half a glass, then lit another cigarette from the stub in his mouth. He looked at his watch.

Twenty-five of eleven. Bill Hoag had the night-trick but he should be awake by now.

He went back into the bedroom and made a grab for the directory, thumbing through. Once more he dialed.

"Scott Daniels, Bill. You don't sound sleepy. Did I blow reveille?"

"Been up an hour. Wonder I can sleep at all with these kids wrecking the joint. What's on your mind, buddy?"

"You wanna make sergeant? In say a week's time."

"Sure. And the next week captain. You feeling all right?"

"Perfectly sane. I'm dead serious. Now if you personally were to arrest some characters involved in the stick-up of the Second National Bank of Miami, wouldn't that be worth sergeant?"

"It sure would be worth it. I might even get it. Don't crap me now. What would you know about the Second National heist?"

"Not quite everything—but almost. And I want the reward. I might skim off a thousand for some help, though. You wanna talk about it?"

"Damn right! If you're not shoveling it."

"Your place or mine?"

"I better come over there. Too much racket here. Now listen, Scott—I'm in no mood. Are you on the level?"

"I mean it, Bill."

"Gimme about half an hour at the most."

"Okay. See you."

He went out to the kitchen and killed the rest of the beer. He couldn't sit still. He kept pacing from room to room. Smoking furiously, he began to go over the facts as he knew them, one by one. After an age, the doorbell rang.

He went to answer.

EIGHTEEN

SHORTLY AFTER one o'clock, Scott Daniels entered the bank by way of the Commerce Exchange Building. He remained in the Second National less than thirty seconds, just long enough to make one sneaky observation. Clay Scofield was definitely at his desk. For what Scott had in mind it would be a very bad thing if he were not. Further, Scofield would not be leaving again. Scott had called just after noon and the vice president was out to lunch.

In ten minutes Scott was driving over MacArthur Causeway, searching Bayview Drive. It looked as if Scofield had set a trap which was going to snap shut—right around his own neck. And until then, Scott could certainly handle the surveillance of one female by himself.

It had not been as difficult as Scott imagined to convince Hoag that this was not merely the pipe dream of an amateur sleuth. Hoag, a lanky raw-boned man with careful eyes in a craggy face, had listened with riveted attention, interrupting with staccato bursts of speech.

"It all fits," he said finally. "This Scofield must have tipped them on the delivery for a slice of that big green pie. There's just one rub. It takes more than a hatful of probabilities to haul in vice presidents of banks. You know the score. And I know it. But we need evidence that you can hold right here in your mitt. Now if we could take Scofield and his woman in on any decent charge at all, then we could sweat them down. I need to get in that Bayview place and look around. And it seems like you're going to be my excuse. Because obviously the bastard is laying for you."

Hoag had loaned Scott his own private weapon, a stubby .32 revolver, telling him not to use it except in the most extreme emergency.

According to Hoag, a policeman was on duty twenty-four hours a day. And with a catch in view coveted by the whole department, Hoag wanted to make the arrest without the aid of fellow officers. For this much he would take credit, all other awards tangible and intangible, except a thousand dollars, going to Scott.

The plan had been set. From four o'clock onward, Hoag, driving an unmarked police car, would be parked in sight of the Bayview address. It was naturally assumed that Scofield would arrive before the appointed hour and some small fact might be learned by watching him.

Promptly at five o'clock when Scott arrived, and while Scofield's attention was drawn to him, Hoag would take a circuitous route on foot and approach the house from the rear. He would then hide himself in a position where he could, if not see, at least hear. For it was a day of molten heat and certainly widows must be left open. In the event of a climactic situation, Scott was to raise his voice in severe protest, his words acting as a cue. However, Scott himself would be armed and ready.

Whatever the situation, Hoag would be prepared. He had most efficient and silent devices for opening doors and cutting window glass. And if the very unexpected occurred, there was always the police radio.

Hoag was a cop of the widest experience and Daniels had congratulated himself that he had not tried to be a hero and make any brave captures himself. He was not so foolish as to be unafraid of desperate people, however cloaked in the raiment of the non-professional criminal.

In spite of this, he was not without the necessary guts to do a small job on his own initiative. And no sooner had Hoag left him than a startling thought struck him. Scofield must have come to the conclusion that since Scott would recognize Valerie the minute he laid eyes on her and be alarmed, it would be wise to have her in hiding. She might even be sent to some other place before the meeting and possibly escape altogether.

And where was Roy Whalen if he was the second of the two gunmen? Likely he never went north and would therefore be available to help Scofield with his trap. In which case the odds might not be so good.

Scott had tried frantically to reach the detective, but Hoag could not be found. So at the moment he was on his way to make a cautious check of the Bayview address to see if there was evidence of anyone at home. Then, from his car, he would keep watch until Hoag arrived and report his findings. To phone the number again would be risky. If Valerie answered, a second fake call would place her on guard immediately.

He found Bayview Drive after a short delay because Scofield had neglected to tell him the name of the isle upon which the street was located. But after doubling back and inquiring at a gas station, he found it easily enough. Winding over that pleasant, innocuous-seeming drive with its handsome bower of palms and costly dwellings, he was somewhat surprised to find that 3728 was the most unassuming of them all. Scofield had more property than house.

He slid by without changing speed and caught the picture out of the corner of his eye. No car in front of the house or near it, carport empty. A feeling, without real basis in fact, of desertion. But surely if someone other than Valerie were there, a car would be present.

Valerie McLean. Who in God's name was she? From what corner of life and the world did she come?"

He swung around the next block, turned and parked so that he had a good oblique view of the house. He sat smoking, trying to decide on the next step. He looked at his watch. Quarter of two. And two hours and fifteen minutes to Bill Hoag.

He studied the grounds. A hedge of hibiscus some seven feet tall at the sides, open at front and rear. An abundance of scrub palms and vegetation, an immense poinciana tree. Plenty of concealment if the approach was right. Neighboring house on the right side, his side, shuttered. More than half the houses shuttered. Gone north for the hot months.

No one came or went and after a short time, he became unbearably restless in the heat of the car. If even Valerie wasn't there. . . . Bad. But sweet possibility for inspection.

He flipped his cigarette and got out of the car. He walked back a ways, then crossed the street. On this side, with an island of palms dividing the road, his approach would be screened. He moved forward, past the dangerous corner and out of sight. He cut left up the next block, a street removed. When he was in back of the house with the shutters, the neighboring one to 3728, he walked up someone's drive to the rear of their house. He found himself on the edge of a swimming pool. A plump woman in bathing suit sunned herself on a reclining chair, eyes closed.

She sat up, startled. He was going to retreat but changed his mind.

"Sorry," he said. "Guess I'm lost. Looking for Bayview Drive."

The small shadow of fear left her face and she smiled, pointing.

"Next block, young man. Right over there."

"Thank you. Mind if I cut through your property? It's just too hot to go around."

"Oh, that's perfectly all right. You go right on." With another brief show of teeth, she fell back and closed her eyes.

He passed through to the shuttered house and from it to the hedge. He made a narrow opening and looked upon the backyard. Trees, outdoor furniture, a barbecue pit. No sign of anyone. He scanned the back windows. Blinds drawn on all of them, but something odd. He made a more careful study.

There! One of the windows was broken. It was a large, three-section window of the awning type. More than half of the lower section was gone. It must have been a recent break, for a piece of cardboard was crudely fixed in the jagged opening.

Never, thought Scott, would there be a better opportunity to search the house. Providing, of course, that it was empty. The money itself might be there. Or a clue to the hiding place. Any way you looked at it, there had to be some kind of usable evidence in that house. An unbelievable chance to find it.

Yet, it was dangerous. It seemed absolutely necessary to be sure the house was vacant. But how? How! A guess wasn't good enough.

After a moment he got an idea, discarded it, came back to it. Why not? The window was already broken. Later he would pick up the glass and with the blind drawn, it wouldn't be discovered for some time.

He searched around the yard of the shuttered house and brought back several fair-sized stones from a rock garden. He made a sufficient opening in the hedge and drew back his hand. Again he hesitated. The hell with it. He had a gun and concealment. Small boys could be blamed for throwing rocks. He took careful aim. He hurled the stone. It fell short by a foot and struck cement with hardly a sound.

A second try also missed. But on the third, the remaining fragment of glass exploded with a rewarding crash and tinkle that would be twice amplified within.

He waited, watching from the screen of hedge, barely parted.

Not a single blind disturbed. No one came to the door, And in that nervous house a whisper of disturbance would need investigating.

He clocked off another couple of minutes and stepped through the hedge. Hand on the gun in his pocket, he crossed to the window and listened. Satisfied, he squeezed into the opening, pushed aside the blind and a section of torn screen, dropped to the kitchen floor.

He tiptoed. On soundless feet, gun in hand, he moved from the dining area into the living room. Empty. Everywhere, slats of venetian blinds were slanted downward, giving light but privacy from the exterior. Tensely, he moved from a bedroom to a bath to another bedroom. He had been right.

The house was empty.

He put the gun in his pocket and returned to the kitchen. Quickly he cleaned up all but a few tiny shards of glass and dumped the fragments into a garbage can just outside the kitchen door. He went back to the one bedroom which looked in use.

Double-bed with a yellow spread—neat. A couple of small chairs. A vanity, dresser and mirror, beige carpet wall-to-wall and . . . Where the carpet came out from under the bed by one of twin night tables, a large irregular stain, faded by much scrubbing. Blood? No time for speculation.

He began to open drawers, finding only female garments in the vanity, male in the dresser. He went to one of two closets and discovered an array of dresses and shoes, fine quality. He was headed for the second when he had a strange feeling of presence in the room.

He froze in stride and slowly turned his head. His gaze fastened on the doorway.

Framed in the center with a curious look of placid watchfulness was Valerie McLean.

She was dressed in slacks and a white jersey which followed snugly the lift and thrust of her breasts. She wore tennis sneakers. Though she was rigidly immobile, she leaned on the doorframe with apparent casualness.

Slowly he let the gun sink back into his pocket and removed his hand. He didn't know what to say except, "Hello, Valerie."

"It took you a long time," she said.

"Not so long. A few days."

"How you must have worked at it," she said, still unmoving. "And how clever you must have been."

"I had luck here and there. Or I might never have found you."

"How clever," she said again. "And how foolish."

"Foolish?"

"Why couldn't you tend to your own silly life and let others live theirs the way they have to live it?"

"Have to?"

"Have to. We do what we have to do." Her voice broke and trembled on the edge of breaking. "I feel sorry for you," she said.

"For me?"

She nodded. "And for me, and for—for everyone."

She made no sense at all. "Where were you just now?" he said. "I know the house was empty. Where did you come from?"

"In the front door," she said, her voice gaining control.

"And before that?"

"Does it matter?"

"Are you alone?" His hand went back to the pocket.

"You don't see anyone else, do you?"

"It's the ones I don't see that worry me."

"If I wasn't alone, you would have known it before now."

"Just the same, we'll look around," he said, and this time the gun came out of his pocket.

She looked at the gun with small interest. "How thoughtful to be always prepared."

"Just walk ahead of me and make the tour, Valerie."

Behind her, he went from room to room. He looked outside, front and back.

"Now," he said. "We'll start with the other bedroom and we'll take everything out of the drawers and closets. You'll do the work, I'll watch."

With a shrug, she preceded him. As they went from room to room, she silently opened the emptied drawers and closets just as he ordered. Her attitude was stoic, resigned. He found nothing incriminating in any corner of the house. They returned to the living room and he sat down facing her with the gun restored to his pocket.

"Well," he said. "I didn't really expect to find the money. But I did expect to find some little thing. It's over, Valerie. Completely over. Why don't you just tell me?"

"I never seem to know when a thing is over," she said. "That's my trouble. Would you mind giving me a hint as to what got you started on all this?"

"I was watching in the mirror when you opened the suitcase. Very few honest people can get that much cash together."

"I see. Very stupid of me. But I was so upset." She laughed without humor. "In a way, I paid you five hundred dollars to hunt me down."

"Oh, I'll return it," he said. "But not to you. What happened to Roy Whalen, Valerie?"

Her face underwent the first real change.

"Don't look so startled. I have most of the facts. He and Marty Bates did it together. With Scofield's help, of course. Isn't that right?"

"I only listen."

"You don't seem the type for this, Valerie. What are you all about? I'm really curious."

"You know what they say about curiosity, don't you?" The question came from another part of the room and the voice which asked it was distinctly male.

Clayton Scofield stood in the archway of the dining alcove. The round cold mouth of the .45 in his fist dared Scott to move for his own gun. He didn't.

"Oh, thank God!" sighed Valerie. "I thought you'd never get here."

"Your call caught me with a customer waiting. I had to lend him some money to get rid of him. He was a very bad risk."

She got up and went towards him.

"No," he said. "Don't get in my way."

She paused. "He's got a gun," she said.

"Is that so? Stand up, Daniels. And step away from the chair."

He obeyed.

"Get the gun, Valerie. Walk around him and reach from behind. That's it."

Fingers groped and found the .32. She delivered it and it disappeared in Scofield's pocket.

"Sit down again, Daniels," Scofield ordered.

"How did you know I was here, Valerie?" asked Scott from the chair. His own voice sounded immensely calm while his palms were fear-damp.

"Luck," she said with a wry smile. "I was bored and I had gone for a walk. I was just rounding a corner and there you were getting out of the car. I ducked back and watched until you were out of sight. Then I went in and called Clay. While I was talking to him, I heard the back window crash and I went out the front door."

"I told you to stay outside and wait for me," said Scofield. "You were taking a chance."

"I wanted to keep him busy," she said. "I was afraid he'd leave."

"Well," Scofield said, "this doesn't change anything. It only convinces me he's a very bad boy to have around."

"He knows much more than we dreamed," said Valerie. "He knows about Marty. And he knows about Roy, too."

"Nonsense!" said Scofield. "If he knew you killed Roy he would have brought the police with him."

"Oh God, oh God," she moaned. "He didn't know Roy was dead, just that he helped."

"What difference does it make?" snapped Scofield. "He already knew one thing too many."

"The police know, too," said Scott in the shocked, near whisper which was all he could muster. "Don't try anything with me, Scofield. They know I'm here and they're watching this house."

"Save your breath," said Scofield. "I'm familiar with how the police operate. When they have anything, they move right in and make an arrest. Is that his Ford around the corner, Valerie?"

"Yes. The gray one."

"Let's have the keys, Daniels."

He hesitated.

"Come on, come on!"

He got up, found the keys and began to walk forward with them.

"No you don't," said Scofield. "Throw them. None of your boy-scout ideas will work with me. Just remember that."

Scott gave the keys a toss. Scofield caught them neatly in his left hand and dropped them in his pocket.

"Back in the chair, Daniels."

Scott returned, said quickly, "Listen to me, Scofield. Listen carefully. At thirty-five minutes after ten this morning I called a cop by the name of Hoag, Detective William Hoag. I told him everything I know. He followed me up here. Right at this moment he's out there somewhere, waiting for you to make a move. He had a radio car and he's in touch with headquarters. The smartest thing for you to do is. . . ."

"The smart thing for *you* to do is shut your mouth," said Scofield. "You have a dangerous tendency to make me nervous. You think I came this far just to let a small-time sonofabitch like you wreck everything I've done? Two other flunkies stood between me and a half million. You saw what happened to one of them."

Stall, stall! thought Scott. "And where's the other one?" he said. "Where did you hide Roy Whalen?" If he got an answer to that question, his own fate was certain.

Scofield scratched the lobe of an ear and studied him steadily over the gun. "You must have walked right past his grave," he said. "He's under our neighbor's rock garden, nine feet down."

Valerie sat on the arm of a chair near him. At his words she dropped her head into cupped hands as if to hide her eyes from some agonizing memory. She looked up suddenly. "Clay," she said. "Suppose he's telling the truth. About the police."

"Shut up, shut up!" he barked. "Do you think I'm an idiot? I knew he was lying. When I didn't see you outside I went around the block looking for you, and then over to the next street. There's just one car in this area, his Ford. Empty. And no one on foot."

"But suppose he told his wife he was coming here."

"I did," said Scott.

Scofield ignored him. "You know what I said about that, Valerie. He never got here. I'll be terribly concerned about what happened to him."

Valerie lowered her head again and began to cry softly.

"For God's sake, stop that blubbering!" Scofield shouted.

She looked up slowly. "It was different just talking about it, planning it," she choked. "Roy was really self-defense. But this . . . I can't do it, Clay. I won't let you!"

"You won't let me? You'll do just what you're told!"

"I won't sign for the money in those boxes." Her chin came up. "You'll need my signature."

"You're bluffing, Valerie. I know you. We'll go up to Palm Beach in the morning and you'll sign. And then I'll take charge of the money."

She was silent.

Looking from the barrel of the gun to Scofield's face, Scott Daniels could see only one end to it. All his life he had fought with fear of one kind or another. But this was something else. The guts were sickened and the mind was sucked dry of pride and resistance by the blotting paper of self-preservation. Action was a thing of horse operas, our hero with a sarcastic smile on his face, tossing a lamp at the villian with perfect timing and accuracy, then rushing in to wrest away the big six-shooter. Stuff of the B-movies. He could think of no brave scheme with even a hundred-to-one chance. Hoag miles away somewhere. And Myra, unsuspecting. Myra, Myra. . . .

Scofield moved cautiously around him and got behind his chair. He felt the hard press of the barrel against the back of his head. His thoughts raced wildly. His mind was a slot machine spinning crazily on the last coin of chance, looking for the impossible jackpot of an idea.

His eyes darted about—dining alcove to kitchen and back door—hallway to bath and two bedrooms . . . Valerie seated on the chair arm, her mouth falling open, eyes widening to enormous mirrors reflecting his death . . .

"No!" she screamed.

"Go into the bedroom and shut the door, Valerie." Scofield's voice with the tight quality of a surgeon about to perform an operation of rare consequence.

"Clay, Clay! You're not going to shoot him in cold blood?"

"Don't be foolish, Valerie. I'm merely going to put him to sleep. Quietly. But permanently. Now stay—or get out!"

She ran from the room. The bedroom door slammed.

The pressure of the barrel was released from his head and he understood. The big automatic was being reversed to bring the butt down on his head with bone-crushing force. In that instant of reversal, it was the time, the *only* time.

He whirled, half stood, swung back and upward with all his might. The blow was blind and caught Scofield on the side of the head, but with great force. He reeled sideways, almost fell, recovered. He was holding the .45 by the barrel, but as Daniels charged, swiftly made the switch to his left hand and fired.

The sound boomed and ricocheted off the walls. The bullet went wild, striking glass somewhere with a shattering impact. Scofield had fired, then jumped swiftly out of range of Daniels' fists. He was still off-balance but bringing the gun to bear for a more careful shot.

There was only one course left and Daniels took it without hesitation. He ran zig-zag to the nearest refuge, that hall with its open doors ten steps away.

The second shot might have killed him, but he stumbled and fell headlong. The third shot ripped up flooring by his right shoulder. He was saved from the fourth as Valerie came gasping out of the bedroom into the line of fire.

He heard Scofield shout to her on the run. But by this time, Daniels had scrambled on hands and knees to the nearest cover, the bathroom just beyond. He heaved the door shut and locked it. He squeezed against the wall in that tiny room and looked to the window. It was of opaque glass and large enough to pass a small boy but never a man of his size. There was no escape.

The next shot told him that Scofield had figured the one part of that room where he would seek protection, the corner space near the sink. The bullet plowed in at an angle, struck the tile an inch above his head, bounced and zinged around the room to fall with a thud in the bathtub.

There was now the sound of Scofield shouldering the door, the door shuddering and splintering. Silence. A harsh shout of distant command, followed by another shot, also distant and with less timbre. Then heavy feet on the approaching run and the two words, "Got him!"

The silence which followed was broken only by the sobbing of Valerie McLean. Then a fist pounding on the door and a guttural male voice saying, "Okay, come outta there, buddy. Police officers. We got him!"

Shaking violently, he opened the door and went out.

One uniformed officer was bent over Scofield who lay flat on his back, a widening stain spreading over his stomach.

He was not yet dead but apparently heaving his last few breaths. Weeping, Valerie stood looking down at him.

The other officer, tall and young with a boyish face, watched Daniels come out of the bathroom with an expression of mingled shock and wariness. Then he holstered his service revolver, said, "Christ, oh, Christ. I wouldn't have shot him. But he was bringin' that goddam cannon up on me and I thought he might blow my head off. Who are you, bud?"

"Scott Daniels," he answered on a huge sigh. "Almighty God, but I'm glad to see you. Wouldn't you know that Hoag would figure it out and come through. Hoag sent you, didn't he?"

"Hoag?" said the officer. "Who's he?"

"Detective Bill Hoag."

"Must be another precinct. Don't know the man. We got a call from some jane over in back of here. Said a guy crossed through her property, acting kind of funny. Said she followed and watched him. Said she saw him bust a glass and break into this place. We would of been here sooner but she gets excited, gives us the wrong address and we're two blocks away. Well, I got to phone in for an ambulance. Then we'll all go down to the station. You and the missus can give us a full report."

"Sure," said Scott, looking at Valerie who had turned toward him and was biting the back of her hand, "sure, we'll be very glad to go down to the station and give you the whole story."

"Nothin' to it," said the officer. "The man was shot resisting arrest. Simple case of breaking and entering."

NINETEEN

SCOTT DANIELS gave the boy a coin and shut the door. He began to rip the flap of the telegram as he crossed the living room to Myra. It was two days later on a Sunday afternoon.

The bank story, enshrining his name, had been headlined in the newspapers of the country coast to coast.

"Telegram?" said Myra excitedly. "What is it?"

"New York," he said. "Hold on, I'm reading." He finished, passed her the wire, bent over her chair to study it again.

REPLY EARLIEST CAN DO GUEST SHOT SULL-VAN PROGRAM SUNDAY NEXT. SUGGEST YOU RESIGN PRESENT JOB SHORT NOTICE AS HAVE SEVERAL FREE-LANCE CONTRACTS READY YOUR SIGNATURE PRACTICALLY NAME OWN PRICE. HAPPY HAVE YOU AND MYRA GUESTS OUR PLACE UPON ARRIVAL NEW YORK.
WARMEST PERSONAL REGARDS
MILT LUNDBERG

"Oh, lord!" said Myra. "Isn't that perfectly marvelous!"

"Typical," said Scott. "Absolutely typical. They all love you when you're on top. All is forgiven, come home. No questions asked, just come and bring your shining, new, nationally-advertised-for-free name, and make us a bale of money. Warmest, absolutely guaranteed personal regards, Milt Lundberg."

"Well, of course it's ironic and screamingly obvious," said Myra. "But you're not going to turn it down because you're bitter, are you, dear?"

"Hell, no. I'm going to capitalize on it. I'm damn well going to entrench myself with it. I wouldn't turn it down any more than I turned down that reward." He smiled. "As a matter of fact, I have a sneaking suspicion that in the back of my mind, it was what I meant when I said there was something more important than the money."

Myra nodded. "That and the one reason you're still hiding from yourself."

"What reason?"

"The wish to succeed at something big again without help from anyone. Why do you think you *really* went up to that house ahead of time and alone?"

"Maybe you're right," he said. "I don't know myself as well as you do, hon."

"Well," she said brightening. "We ought to celebrate! Tonight. Because tomorrow you're back on the job."

"Okay. Some place cozy and intimate. Like the Fountainbleu."

"Intimate like Grand Central," said Myra. "But terribly gay and extravagant."

"And before dinner," he continued, "a very dry, beautifully chilled martini. The first in over a year."

Myra frowned, her gamin face trying unsuccessfully to look stern. "Do you think you should do that, dear?"

"I can't see any harm. Every now and then, on special occasions. Although I really don't think it's important, one way or the other."

"In that case," she said, "I just happen to have the mixings for a very dry martini right in the kitchen. One now and another before dinner."

She gave him a pat and with a tongue-in-cheek smile, flounced from the room.

He watched her affectionately until she was out of sight.

Then he picked up the telegram and went to call Western Union.